How Did She Get There?

Ann Karen Dowd

White Ink Press
P.O. Box 635
Remsenburg, N. Y. 11960

ISBN: 0615335306
ISBN-13: 9780615335308

White Ink Press
P.O. Box 635
Remsenburg, New York 11960
editor@whiteinkpress.com

For Terry—

whose love and generosity kept me writing

ACKNOWLEDGEMENTS

Writing *How Did She Get There?* required a leap of faith that for many years I didn't have the courage to make. In 2007, my daughter-in-law, Pauline sent me the book, *The Secret* by Rhonda Byrne for my birthday. I totally embraced the theory of the Laws of Attraction about which *The Secret* is based. The people who "miraculously" showed up in my life as a result of practicing the LOA are those to whom I owe my deepest appreciation and gratitude. They had the faith that I lacked... and much, much more.

I wish to thank Kelly Bookamer, my first LOA coach, for teaching me how to believe in myself, and especially, for her dream about me at the Oscars in a royal blue dress. I can't wait for us to be there! When Kelly retired from coaching, I was blessed to start working with LOA coach, Flavia Daay whose wisdom and unwavering commitment to my vision has guided me along the way to define who I am as a writer and as a person. My appreciation to Alice Peck for seeing the beauty and importance of Caro's story, and whose critique, "I want more," inspired me to develop the short story into a novella. I want to thank Jessica Swift for her encouragement and wonderfully creative insights. My appreciation goes out to Barbara Milbourn for her timely, and meticulous proofreading. To Ted Gilley, I am profoundly grateful. His editorial skills are remarkable; he doesn't miss a trick! He pushed me to become a better and more complete writer. One of Ted's rare compliments made me smile for the rest of the day.

Until the next book...

Ann Karen
April 10, 2010

Love is like the wild-rose briar;
Friendship is like the holly-tree.
The holly is dark when the rose briar blooms,
But which will bloom most constantly?

~EMILY BRONTE

CHAPTER ONE

Caro tiptoed to mute the resounding click-clack of her heels on the marble floor, but not before several family members glared at her with their faces pulled down in a collective frown. Shrinking under their tacit disapproval, she continued walking toward the altar of Saint Anthony's Church as they filed out.

During the memorial service Caro had sat in the back pew with the staff from New Century Publishers, who'd taken time to pay their respects to their veteran editor, Marcie Harrington. Unlike them, Caro wasn't there out of a sense of propriety.

She'd met Marcie twelve years before when New Century bought out its rival, the press responsible for introducing Caro to the literary world with her first book of poetry. Thus, she'd been prepared to hate Marcie for putting her previous editor out of a job. But the unexpected happened. Their relationship gathered momentum from the outset. Before long they were inseparable and Caro came to depend on Marcie's impeccable advice.

Outside of work, they lunged headlong into each other's lives. Caro had squeezed in beside Marcie during New Jersey Nets basketball games. She'd suffered through New York Giants football games even though she was clueless as to the nuances of play. Marcie was at Caro's elbow when Caro's daughter, Abby, had boarded British Air to live in London. Together Caro and Marcie hiked the 146 miles of the Appalachian Trail that wound through the center of Vermont's Green Mountains.

Caro couldn't *now* let Marcie go without getting close to her one more time. The sense of so much stale air between Marcie's spiritless body and Caro's empty heart made her feel weightless, even worse, shiftless. The ordered pattern of her days seemed to have gotten tucked into the pinched corners of the quilting of Marcie's coffin. Personal tasks and job actions, appointment times with the publisher, and venues for book readings had been subject to Marcie's approval. Without her friend's intervention, those agendas would pass in scattered disorder. Marcie was the logician, the organized planner.

As Caro approached the casket, sequins of sunlight from the stained glass windows shimmered over Marcie's flesh. She seemed infused with life, her death a malicious hoax.

She laid her hand on Marcie's and rolled her finger over the braided gold ring that she and her husband, Zach, had given Marcie for her fiftieth birthday. The inscription read: *With unending devotion, Caro & Zach*. Then suddenly overcome with emotion, she backed away. How careless to walk in Morningside Park alone at night! Raised on the Upper West Side, she knew better. Morningside had a worse reputation for muggers than its famous neighbor, Central Park. A blow to the head with a bat and she was gone.

Caro sensed someone's approach. She glanced up to find her publisher shaking his lowered head.

"It's such a tragedy. I know she was like family."

Caro replied without taking her eyes from Marcie's face. "Thanks, Ethan."

The funeral director appeared moments later. "It's time."

"I'll wait for you outside," Ethan said and patted her shoulder.

Carol cupped Marcie's cheek and stared hard at her face, afraid that as soon as she left she'd forget its details. Even though she'd been married to Zach for twenty-four years, after he died his features sometimes blurred in her mind, and occasionally she found herself studying old photos of him to re-ignite her memory.

In the parking lot, the hard heat of the cement burned under the soles of her sandals and she squinted Ethan's form into focus.

"Are you going ahead with the beach house, Caro? My wife's cousin has a friend who is interested in taking over Marcie's half."

The beach house. Caro groaned at the reminder. The summer was the beginning of a year-long sabbatical from her professorship at Columbia University to finish her latest collection of poems, *In Search of Eros*. She and Marcie had planned to spend June through August in Westhampton Beach, Long Island.

"I know it wouldn't be easy, being so soon and all," Ethan said. A ring of perspiration encircled his neck and colored the collar of his shirt. "We didn't want to think of you *not* going. You'll need the change more than ever."

Caro regained her earlier composure. "As much as I appreciate the thought, I'd be horrible company."

"All right then." He stepped in and kissed Caro's cheek.

Throughout the final viewing and service, Caro had wanted to be alone with her misery. Now as she watched Ethan pack his stout body behind the wheel of his Mercedes sports coupe, she leaned forward, about to call him back, but stopped herself. He wasn't who she wanted.

There is one friend in the life of each of us who seems not a separate person, however dear and beloved, but an expansion, an interpretation, of one's self, the very meaning of one's soul.

~EDITH WHARTON

CHAPTER TWO

When Zach had died of a massive coronary five years earlier, the loss had struck Caro in a different way. It had been sharper than her present grief—a razor-blade kind of hurt that caused her to cry for days, hard tears that turned her eyes into burning slits.

For weeks after his funeral, Caro moved through their home with her arms wrapped around herself as if to contain the waves of grief that rose up inside of her. A surprise, really. She had loved Zach, but their marriage was a lopsided affair: in essence, Caro enjoyed the relatively inactive pleasures of reading books on philosophy and ancient history, and listening to classical music in her spare time; Zach built things with his hands and possessed the level-headedness his work as a general contractor demanded.

In fact, they'd met when she hired him to remodel the brownstone apartment her father had left her in his will. He began work at the end of May, as soon as her teaching semester was finished at Columbia University. By the completion of the renovation in September, he'd moved in.

Six months later, after Caro accepted Zach's marriage proposal, he said, "I'll be so proud to call you my wife. There's nothing I won't do to keep you happy."

True to his pledge, Zach accommodated Caro's needs, all in the name of her art. He didn't complain about the consecutive evenings when she closed herself up in her study immediately after supper to work on a particularly difficult poem. He got used to eating breakfast alone on those mornings when she rose from sleep with a new idea and went directly to her computer to get it down before his or Abby's needs infringed on her thoughts. He took their daughter to her ballet lessons and soccer practice on those Saturdays when Caro was stuck grading papers.

Once after a rare argument, when Caro lost track of time and was an hour late picking Abby up from school, Zach said to her, "You're about your work and that's all. Everything and everyone comes second."

Caro's objection dissolved into tears. "I know I make your life difficult sometimes..."

"Difficult," Zach emphasized, "doesn't even begin to cover it. I put up with a lot from you, Caro, but forgetting about Abby is downright negligent."

"That's not fair," Caro protested.

"Oh, yes it is," Zach shot back. "In fact, I'm being gracious about the whole matter."

"Gracious! You're being a goddamn nag."

"That's what I call being accountable for your actions," he said, his voice thick with sarcasm.

As the months passed after his death, Caro's grief lessened and a quickening sense of freedom stirred inside her because she'd known her limitations as a wife and mother. With him gone and Abby in London, she could now work whenever she wanted and enjoy the solitude of her study without guilt. For her, there was no better place to be.

As young as four and five, she'd scripted poems with crayons inside her coloring books, graduating to pens and paper as she got older. As she'd title each small verse and sign her name, she'd imagine herself a famous writer in spite of her parents' rebukes to "stop daydreaming." Her father had been especially callous. "Who do you think you are, Hemingway? People like him are born different. You're no more special than anyone else in this family so get that nonsense out of your head."

Her mother had patted her head and told her to stand up straight. "You'll get married and won't have to write. It's a husband's job to make a living and support his wife. Look at your father."

Caro had accepted what her mother had said as truth because she was happy with him, and Caro had seen the early photographs of her dad as a twenty-eight-year-old upon his arrival at Ellis Island with nothing more than his suitcase. A head taller than most of his Italian compatriots, his large patrician nose seemed to symbolize how she'd come to know him—a proud businessman who'd celebrated his fiftieth birthday with an upscale move to the suburbs and a brand new Mercedes.

Even so, the sense of being a *somebody* never subsided and when Caro read *Little Women* she took to the character of Jo with unabashed enthusiasm. She'd go about her bedroom reciting the lines written for the heroine: "I think I shall write books, and get rich and famous; that would suit me, so that is my favorite dream."

As Caro matured, the inner conflict set up by the juxtaposition of her mother's advice to depend on a man versus her own desire for success and independence, produced a low-grade panic: which path to follow? When she'd met Zach, she tried to tell herself that loving him would suffice.

But the poetry in her head wouldn't let her rest and just as when she was a child, she found herself scribbling verses on whatever odd bits of paper were at hand. She progressed to writing on a laptop, and began submitting her work to literary magazines.

She'd lost count of the rejections she received, but then came the occasional acceptance. For their fifth wedding anniversary, Caro handed her husband a copy of *Poetry Magazine*. "Check out the table of contents," she'd said.

He read, "Three Poems by Caroline Barrone," and his face creased into a grin. How often had he heard her daydream aloud of her name appearing in *Poetry*, one of the most prestigious magazines of its kind?

After that, Caro wanted to maximize the boost in her reputation that inclusion in *Poetry* created. She dedicated more and more hours to her writing in order both to hone her craft and supplement the number and diversity of her poems.

Consequently, when she pondered her recent freedom without Zach, she understood better why she had never questioned his death. She hadn't asked why he had died at so early an age or challenged the universe, asking Why him and not someone else? In fact, her swift acceptance of his passing made her consider that her initial grieving was, to some extent, almost a knee-jerk reaction—society's instruction on how she must respond to her husband's death.

Ultimately, she had to admit she hadn't loved Zach to the depth she'd been avowing all those years. Selfish? Yes. She'd banked her love like gold bullion in a vault, doling it out only when she saw fit, for fear that squandering her feelings would compromise her art.

Abby's reaction was so much more appropriate, and for that, Caro was envious. Zach died in February. In March, Caro traveled to London and stayed with Abby for three weeks. She remembered several conversations with her daughter while the girl was still trying to make sense of her father's death. "I'm mad, Mom. I know shit happens, but why to our family? Why *my* dad?"

"I don't know," was all Caro could reply. Her inability to feel the same kind of anger that Abby experienced had exasperated her daughter. Theirs was a relationship that for the most part had moved forward because of Zach. He'd mediated many disagreements between mother and daughter.

When Caro had returned to New York she'd lamented to Marcie, "I feel you're the only person I can talk to who's not out to criticize or judge, or tell me how I failed in the mother department."

And Marcie had listened as always, because although Zach had been uncomplaining about taking care of many household and parental duties, Caro went to Marcie for her emotional needs. Zach liked to fix things. If Caro vented to him, he'd feel compelled to find a solution when all she wanted was for him to listen. Marcie would let Caro talk herself out. Whatever comments Marcie might make, they were supportive even on the occasions she disagreed.

Now without Marcie, Caro felt shattered and alone.

Caro wasn't normally a cathartic poet. She believed diaries were nothing more than illusory narratives that tethered a person to the past. But she needed to resurrect Marcie on the page, and so she indulged herself an hour of journaling. She began with her first impression of Marcie on the morning Ethan had introduced them.

2 June

I remember...Marcie behind her desk—large hands for a woman—splayed on the rosewood surface...brash, unforgiving voice dictating commands into the speakerphone. Haunting eyes— memorable for their ability to rebuke with their color alone—hard, dark mahogany. Same color hair— bottle-dyed—too long for her age, especially the bangs. Brooks Brothers suit… The high kick pleat showed off her legs. Zach would have been impressed.

"This is Caroline Barrone," Ethan said.

"I normally welcome authors with long-term intentions," Marcie said. "But I know how I'd feel if a new editor was being forced on me due to publishing power plays. We own your contract for your current book. After that, it's up to you if you stay or go."

Rigid in the overstuffed leather chair…she buttonholed me with her gaze. My previous editor had been warmhearted, a poet in her own right.

An hour later, Marcie ended the meeting with, "My secretary will set up our appointment schedule."

Then…in an unimagined gesture, she picked up my manuscript… opened to a page she had bookmarked. When she read, her voice undulated in meticulous rhythm.

you whose absence
is an everlasting presence—
fallen to a higher crown
fallen woman
crowned in conception—
your body
my soul
your milk
is the ink
of my poems.

"'The Magdalene Poem.' It's so evocative. A personal favorite," Marcie said.

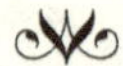

Caro stilled her fingers and rested them on the keyboard. She remembered the mental readjustment that had taken place after Marcie's reading. "The Magdalene Poem" was a personal favorite of Caro's as well.

Although not a religious person in the traditional sense, Caro was devoted to the Blessed Mother. It was a dedication that began in preparation for her confirmation into the Catholic Church when she had to pick a patron saint to emulate and be named after. Not one to cause hurt feelings, her juvenile logic was to choose the head of all the saints, the mother Mary. Before long, praying to her divine Mother became a nightly habit that seemed to quell any disappointments from the day.

For inspiration, however, she turned to Magdalene, a woman of literature and legend, politics and theology, controversy and conflict. She was the woman from whom Jesus cast out evil spirits, and then sent her on her way, redeemed. Caro took comfort in Magdalene's story because it showed God's unquestionable mercy no matter how grave the sin.

In spotting and savoring that brief poem, Marcie had acknowledged Caro's core connection to the infamous Magdalene. Caro's gratefulness for Marcie had begun at that moment and never waned.

Caro stood and stretched, her back stiff in objection to her prolonged and intense posture while typing. When she was seated again she re-read the paragraphs of her labor, and for the thousandth time asked, How could she be dead? From the beginning, Marcie had seemed indestructible. Overwhelmed by the depths of her love for her friend, Caro pushed away from the computer and dropped her face into her upturned palms.

Whenever Caro had writer's block and needed inspiration, she headed to the New York Public Library, where on several occasions within its iconic walls she'd come across an artifact, quotation, or snippet of prose that had kindled her imagination. Thus, after a restless night puzzling out the different aspects of love she'd had with Zach and Marcie, she headed downtown.

On the subway, she recalled a Sunday morning after she and Zach had made love. Their pleasure in each other had been unexpectedly satisfying; yet what marked the experience for Caro was the connectedness she'd felt in the aftermath of their sex, the ease that came with being with the same man for twenty-five years.

Marcie had slept over that same weekend. After breakfast on Sunday she and Caro, still wearing their pajamas, had made themselves cozy on the wingback chairs in the den with mugs of coffee. Marcie had recounted the particularly poignant story of her parents' meeting during the Second World War. She'd wept a bit and in those moments of listening, as Caro wiped the tears from her friend's cheek, she'd felt an intimacy with Marcie that rivaled what she'd felt with Zach just a couple of hours before.

Caro recalled how pretty Marcie had looked in the glow of the burgeoning sun, her skin damp from her tears. She'd felt a sudden burst of love for Marcie, so much so that she wanted to take her in her arms with a promise to be with her forever.

Wasn't this love as enduring and soulful as the physical bond she shared with Zach? More so, perhaps, because Caro connected with Marcie on an emotional level that she'd never reached with him.

So what was the best kind of love: the sexual one with Zach, or the platonic love she felt for Marcie, which for her, seemed ever more lasting?

When Caro arrived at the library, she went directly to the philosophy section and began cruising the stacks. She browsed first through works by those men who came readily to mind in the Eastern and Western traditions, from Confucius to Nietzsche.

She'd been at her task for several hours and was preparing to go home when she noticed Plato's *Symposium*, a text she hadn't opened since a Philosophy 101 course in her sophomore year at Vassar College. The professor hadn't spent more than two class periods on it, but the sight of the title now sparked hazy recollections of an unfulfilled interest. She slid the thin volume from the shelf.

Scrunched up in bed that night with the book resting on her knees, her thoughts percolated with the rich fabric of ancient Greek life. She remembered that the Greek word for love—*paiderastia*—was derived from *pais*, the word for boy and *eran*, the verb meaning to love. The Greek idea of beauty was embodied in the young male.

Love, for the sagacious Greeks, had nothing to do with sex, which was forbidden as being an unworthy distraction, something to be performed with women only for the purpose of procreation. Beauty in its purest form was the key to Platonic love, and thus attained only between men—the lovers, and their male students, the beloveds—in a joint pilgrimage of knowledge.

Caro flattened the book on her lap and passed her finger along the inside seam. The more she read, the more the message appealed to her.

It was true that she had searched for everlasting love with Zach and came up short since Marcie's death made a greater impact on her psyche. In addition to the demands she put on him for her career, she and Zach had been complacent, relying on their common habits and Abby's comings and goings to keep equilibrium in their marriage.

Caro adored Marcie. But even when she was still alive, Caro felt that she was missing something along the way with her, as well. At one point after Zach died, Caro had even discussed the possibility with Marcie of the two of them living together. She'd said to Marcie, "We get along, are both alone, and we already refer to the guest bedroom as M's room. You probably have half your wardrobe over here already."

Marcie had begun shaking her head even before her words came out. "I can't do that. I'd feel like I was taking Zach's place somehow."

"How can you think that? He was my husband. Of course, I'm not going to argue the point."

"No, it's fine," Marcie had said. "It's a gracious offer. But I think we both need our own separate spaces."

"It was just an idea," Caro had said. Nothing was ever mentioned again about Marcie moving in.

Caro looked at the clock: five-thirty. Her daughter would be just waking up.

Abby picked up on the second ring. "Mom, you're calling so early."

"Yeah, sorry about that. I…I was thinking about Marcie, and then Dad, and that got me thinking to call and say good morning before you started getting ready for work."

"Good morning to you, too," Abby said. "I'm glad you did. Nice way to start my day."

"So how was your date with Phillip the other night?" Phillip was her daughter's latest boyfriend.

"He's giving me all kinds of grief about turning thirty. Did I tell you that I'm older than him by eight months?"

Caro chuckled. "No, you didn't. But that's not exactly a disastrous amount of time. Besides, from the photos you e-mailed, you look adorable together."

"I'm anxious for you to meet him," Abby said.

"That's a hopeful sign since I'm not coming until the end of August."

"I know, but we've been on more dates in two months than I've had with any other guy. I think he's very special."

"And the feeling is mutual?" Caro asked.

"Yes," Abby said. "Sounds strange, but it's as if we feel driven to be with each other. And then there's the constant coincidences."

"Like?" Caro asked.

"Like him calling at the same moment I have my hand on the phone to dial him. Or having the same thought at the same time. Or showing up at the same place unplanned."

By the tenor of her voice Caro could tell that her daughter must have been smiling. "I'm so happy for you, Abby, and I look forward to meeting him. He will make your birthday extra wonderful this year."

"Get your airline reservations yet?" Abby asked. "We're already planning the party. Going to be a big bash."

"Not yet." Caro squeezed her eyes shut and waited for her daughter's reproach.

"Mom, you know what you're like. Don't disappoint me, okay?"

"Promise, I won't. I'll make them today."

Caro heard the BBC news commentator in the background.

"Got to get going, Mom."

"Sure, Hon. Have a good day."

"You too. I mean night."

Caro fell back on her pillows, suddenly tired. She was envious in a way. Pleased for her daughter but, yes, envious. "Abby and Phillip," she said aloud. How wonderful new love was!

And then just at the moment Caro decided not to think anymore, the answer to her previous questions about love came to her. The solution was that one couldn't come to love casually or with reservation. As with Abby in her relationship with Phillip, underneath the giddy excitement she sounded driven, her voice seemed to carry purpose and direction. Love didn't just come to her; she came to *it*.

Caro sighed. "Perfect love." Next time she'd make it work. Another sigh transformed into a yawn. And then, sleep.

Friends can be said to "fall in like"
with as profound a thud
as romantic partners fall in love.

~LETTY COTTIN POGREBIN

CHAPTER THREE

If Marcie had been alive, she and Caro would have driven out to the beach house on Saturday and enjoyed the festivities the Hamptons offered to celebrate the Memorial Day holiday. But the mere thought of throngs of happy-go-lucky vacationers made Caro want to cry, so she arranged a Tuesday arrival with the realtor. By then, most of the tourists would have gone home, leaving only the weekend husbands to drive west toward their jobs and New York flats, as she headed east.

Marcie had acquired the rental from Gwen Henderson, a friend of a friend who was traveling through Europe for the summer and needed house-sitters. She glanced again at the photo of the house Gwen had sent.

Located on Dune Road in the village of Westhampton, the house was oceanfront. That fact alone made Caro grin as she crossed over one of the bridges that attached Dune Road to the mainland.

A paved strip of land and fragile dunes that ran the length of a barrier island defined by beach, ocean, and salt marshes, the island's shores had been inundated since the 1980s by Wall Street millionaires. Consequently, Dune Road hosted an eclectic mix of architecture ranging from steel-embellished post-modern estates to 1920s cottages gone black with age.

Number 83 was a fern-green Arts and Crafts structure sitting behind a white stucco monstrosity. Caro acknowledged the chauffeur who was wiping down a Bentley and drove the remaining four hundred yards to the house. She passed alongside a dense row of red cedars, which separated the two properties.

The bungalow was typical of its style: one-and-a-half stories with a long, sloping roofline and a wide overhang that seemed nestled into the earth. This earthen tie was exaggerated by a foundation and pillars made of river rock that broadened at the base; the screened-in porch sat low on the dune.

Because the house was situated on a high rise, the ocean was out of sight of the circular driveway. Caro stepped out of the car and the sea air grabbed her hair and ballooned out her caftan top like the wings of a giant sting ray. The smell and sound and the salty taste of it made her spread her arms and breathe deep through her nose.

She stripped off her sandals, tossed them on the porch, and scuttled up the dune by a slim path cut through the cattails and leggy reed grasses. The sand, in early June, was cool. Her feet sunk into it almost to her ankles and she was practically on all fours when she reached the top.

A hodgepodge of blankets, coolers, and umbrellas defined the boundaries of miniature islands of humanity that ran the length and breadth of the shoreline: mothers with children whose juvenile voices leaped above the din of the breakers; rich twenty- and thirty-year-old women in bikinis; their older counterparts under wide-brimmed hats reading romance novels alongside their gray-haired husbands.

Caro shaded her eyes against the sun as she followed a pair of gulls diving for some bit of food. A queue of roadrunners, intent on baby hermit crabs, skittered their way in a zigzag across the sand.

The tableau typified the Hamptons. It was the kind of day that Marcie had valued for her ability to afford renting in a luxury resort area after a career of establishing her worth in the publishing industry. Caro knew from Ethan that this year was to be particularly notable because he had planned to make Marcie a partner. She died without knowing she had achieved her most ambitious goal.

Caro gave in to a snivel and her eyes teared for the life that Marcie had lost as well as for her own feeling of emptiness. She knew that Marcie wouldn't want her to brood. Yet Caro passed several minutes staring at two women engaged in energetic conversation before she could turn away and tromp back down the other side of the dune to unload the car.

Inside the bungalow, a departure from the traditional Arts and Crafts design revealed expansive sheets of glass that opened up the interior. Caro's heart raced at the sight of the vast ocean; the surging surf that seemed to spill at her feet and confuse the boundaries between inside and outside.

She opened the sliding French doors. Halfway in and halfway out the door, Caro suddenly felt bisected, cut through the middle: middle-aged, adrift in the mid-ocean of mourning, in the middle of a book, *In Search of Eros*, her collection of poems whose beginning she could scarcely remember and an ending she could not foresee.

Glancing over her shoulder into the recesses of the great room, the solidity of the wooden architecture soothed her melancholy, while the sunlight that splashed like giant puddles onto the polished pine floor made her smile.

On the deck, she squinted to a point on the horizon where she wanted to believe Marcie was looking back at her from the thin crease between sea and sky.

Later that evening Caro ate sushi in town on the porch of an 1800s converted cottage. The tiny restaurant was situated between a liquor store and barber shop and across from a gourmet deli and an antiques shop—the extent of the storefronts that was considered the community's main street.

After dinner she bought wine and a few food staples, taking the opportunity to introduce herself to business owners, and then went home. She was glad that she'd unpacked and stowed everything away upon arrival; now she could enjoy her first night in contented orderliness.

So thinking, she yanked on an old sweatshirt of Zach's that she refused to throw away; the fabric was at the baby-soft stage that only comes after hundreds of washings. She poured a glass of chardonnay and made her way barefoot down the steps and along the salt-worn catwalk to the beach.

It was too early in the season for mosquitoes and the air was benign. A sailboat in the far distance crossed her line of vision, its lights glittering in the coming dusk. She breathed in the pungent smells of the ocean and sipped her wine, letting the corn silk-colored liquid roll against her teeth.

Caro settled into a welcome reverie. Even after she projected mental images of Marcie she managed to maintain an inner calm. This night was for taking the best of what the moment had to offer.

She remembered a day when she and Marcie had hunted the East Village for a late-nineteenth-century reticule. It was to be a wedding gift from Marcie for her niece to fulfill the "something old" custom of giving. After a full day of rummaging through vintage clothing stores, Caro spotted a particularly delicate one, embroidered with lace and seed pearls.

"Perfect!" Marcie pronounced and purchased it.

Worn out from schlepping the city blocks from East Fourteenth Street to Houston, the north and south boundaries for the Lower East Side, they'd stopped into a bar to relax over drinks.

They'd ordered then sunk into comfy chairs in peaceful retreat. After a few minutes, Marcie kicked Caro's foot under the table and nodded to a pair of women kissing over bottles of Guinness. Caro scanned the room: two more women were sitting shoulder to shoulder in a booth, one of them with her arm slung around the other. A college-aged girl behind them read to her companion from *Curve Magazine*.

"I love this. Stumbling into a gay bar. What are the chances?" Marcie whispered in Caro's ear. "It's so...trendy."

Caro frowned. "I think some of these women would take offense at the notion of being considered *trendy*."

"Oh, don't get on your soap box. I only meant that, well..." She paused and then blurted, "I'm a post-middle-aged divorcee who hasn't been out on a date in ages."

"That's your own fault. You could have gone out last week with that literary agent Ethan brought around. He seemed really into you," Caro said.

"He was ten years my junior," Marcie retorted. "But that's not the point. What I'm saying is that it's just different being here and I like the feel of *difference*. Makes my social life seem less limited."

Caro noted a seldom-heard vulnerability in Marcie's voice, and asked if she'd ever thought about being with another woman sexually.

"No. I told you I'm just feeling...out of touch. I'm not looking to change my sexual preference. I like men."

"I have...thought about it. Actually, I thought a lot of women did at one time or another. Seems almost natural to me, like masturbation."

Marcie screwed up her face in distaste. "Masturbation—"

"Well, have you ever?" Caro coaxed.

"I'm not saying."

"Oh, for Pete's sake, we're best friends. Tighter than tight. If you can't talk about this stuff with me, than who?"

"With no one, that's who," Marcie said flatly.

Caro playfully cuffed Marcie on the arm. "Did I ever tell you that you can be a pain-in-the-butt prude sometimes?"

Marcie nodded.

"So I guess that means you don't want to talk about orgasms either, or S&M?"

"No, and no," Marcie said, and signaled the waitress for another drink.

"Well, I like it here," Caro said in a contented tone. "Makes me feel safe being surrounded my women. Very Sapphic. And that, my dear, is my last word on the subject..."

A fruit fly buzzing around Caro's ear interrupted her daydream just as a masculine voice addressed her.

"Excuse me. Hello."

Caro looked up. She first registered the man's basso voice and lopsided smile, touches of gentility that countered his shaved head and the matching dagger tattoos on his forearms. A woman was with him. A camera with a zoom lens bumped against her chest as she leaned into her companion and slung her arm around his neck. Her skin was glossy with a dark tan gotten only from dedicated baking; the tangled length of her hair was caught up in a scruffy pony tail.

"Tommy and Nina Winters," the man said, nodding to his wife. "We've been waiting for you."

Caro got up, wiped herself of sand and shook their hands. "Caro Barrone."

"Tommy should explain. Gwen heard from the real estate woman you were coming this afternoon. Great to have you! Gwen wanted someone nice who'd take care of the place," Nina offered congenially.

"Settled in yet?" Tommy asked.

"Pretty much. I kept to the bare minimum. Which is yours?" Caro asked, indicating the line of houses that extended along the beach in both directions.

Tommy pointed to the neighboring three-story structure with a lighthouse-inspired tower.

"It's an incredible design," Caro said, appreciative of outstanding architecture from years of studying plans that Zach had brought home for her opinion.

"My brother," Nina said. "When we decided to build, he invited us to Cape Cod to see the one he'd designed on the bay. I have a special thing for lighthouses and the stories they tell."

"We both fell in love," Tommy said. He put his arm around Nina's waist. "Listen, next time you're at the library check out the local author section. *She's* got a coffee-table book out called *Lighting the Way from Bar Harbor to Key West*. The photos taken in North Carolina along the Outer Banks are my favorites."

Nina gave her husband's arm an affectionate hug. "It's self-published and never made a dime."

"It made a few dollars," Tommy said.

"Hah!" Nina's eyes darkened. "Enough to take you out to McDonald's."

"Don't get that way, Baby."

Caro's mental vision flashed back to Zach showing off one of her books. Like Tommy about Nina's photography, Zach had been proud to say that his wife was a poet.

Tommy changed the subject. "By the by, if you need a hairdresser while you're here, come see me. I have a salon and spa in Southampton on Meetinghouse Lane."

Caro resisted the urge to touch her hair as she imagined the grey roots that had inched up the brown dye; she was weeks overdue for an application. "I will," she said in a small voice.

A stiff breeze skidded off the ocean and Caro saw Nina shiver in her midriff top. "It's getting chilly and I'm beginning to feel the effects of moving in—I better go in. But thanks for introducing yourselves."

"Enjoyed it." With their arms linked at their backs, they began to walk away and then Tommy swung them back around. "We have Nina's niece with us for awhile, so if you see a thirteen-year-old hanging out, it's her."

"What's her name?" Caro asked.

"Livia."

Nina warned, "She's very shy so don't be insulted if she doesn't talk the first few times."

"I won't," Caro replied and then watched the couple climb the catwalk that led up the dune to their house.

Caro went inside as well, ready to settle in for the night. The space she lived in was important to her and the bungalow had met her every expectation. In her condo in New York the most important rooms—her bedroom and study—were appointed with infinite care and detail. Believing that she'd been born a century too late, she felt most at home among Victorian furnishings: Persian rugs, Tiffany lamps, and tufted fabrics in warm reds and chocolates.

Thus it was surprising to her that she found these Bahamian seaside tones of apricot, peach, and seaweed green so charming. Gwen's tastes were eclectic, however, and Caro had chosen the smaller of the two guest rooms for her bedroom that was painted in lavender.

Gwen even had arranged for a bouquet of fresh lavender to be brought in for Caro's arrival. So infused was the room in the purple flower that Caro's mood at once eased, and it wasn't long before she was nested in the floral linens. Even after she flicked off the lights, she felt the fabric's blooms envelop her in the invisible arms of safety and comfort.

Is there no way out of the mind?

~SYLVIA PLATH

CHAPTER FOUR

Caro dragged a canvas chair the length of the catwalk, then down a short flight of steps. The near-empty beach was a balm to her melancholic mood; she had had a repeating dream of Marcie the night before.

The dream began the same way with her and Marcie hiking on rough mountainous terrain up a narrow trail that dropped off on either side to several hundred feet below. Being in the lead, Caro doesn't realize immediately that Marcie stops walking in order to let a hiker pass by who'd come up behind her. Instead of continuing on the path, however, he turns to Marcie and accuses her. "You've kidnapped my wife."

"No," Marcie says. "I haven't kidnapped anyone. I don't even know you."

"Yes, there," he insists and points to Caro.

"She's not your wife. She's my friend. Go away! Go on your way."

The man is large and inches Marcie toward the edge.

Caro shouts, "Get away from her!"

"Come to me and I will," the man says.

Caro steps toward him.

The man says, "Good wife," to Caro, and then turns to Marcie and with both arms shoves her over the side.

Caro screams, "No!" She runs at the man and begins to hammer his chest with her fists. "You shouldn't have done that. She was my best friend. You shouldn't have killed her."

"Too late," the man cackled. "Like always, you were too late."

Caro woke up every time at this point in the dream to the heaviness of Marcie having died all over again, and the illogical sense of guilt that she had some culpability in Marcie's death for not being in the park with her the day she was killed.

She looked out over the beach and shook her head, a motion to clear out her brain of Marcie's image. Only a few brave hearts who weren't bothered by the cool temperature lay out in bathing suits. The others, like her, dressed in sweatpants and jackets.

Before long, however, the noonday sun burned down into the sand and sent a pleasurable heat up through her body. Caro sank down in the chair and gave herself up to the cacophony of the gulls' cries as they executed flawless dives in search of food, the hum of a lone fruit fly, and the low slapping of the waves as they licked the edges of the shore.

Her sadness slowly transformed itself as her memory wrapped around the familiarity of this beach. She'd not known the allure of yellow heat and tumbling surf until her sister, Tereza, married Sean, a contractor she met while visiting a college friend. After the wedding Sean built a home for them in the neighboring hamlet of Remsenburg, an unimposing suburb away from the smog and hustle of Manhattan.

Only thirteen when her sister married at nineteen, Caro had had the luxury of summering on the Island. Her brother-in-law was happy to have company for his relocated wife. In the mid-Sixties, the Hamptons, especially Westhampton, traditionally considered the poor sister of its more affluent southern and eastern siblings, had yet to be "discovered." Duck and potato farms were still measured in hectares and spanned the Island from the Atlantic on the north fork to Peconic Bay on the south.

Caro was old enough to be helpful around the house and young enough not to cause any concerns with borrowing the family car. And dating wasn't a worry either until Caro developed a crush on a sixteen-year-old boy, the son of a local policeman. They got caught parking in an off-limits area on the beach in his jeep on a couple of occasions until Sean threatened to send Caro home to New Jersey if she didn't stop seeing him. Tereza tried to intervene on her sister's behalf but Sean remained firm. In word, Caro complied; in reality, she found ways to date the boy behind her brother-in-law's back.

Oftentimes, Caro, Tereza and Sean set out with baskets after he came home from work. He'd gas up the motorboat and they'd head across the Sound to a stretch of beach kept private due to its inaccessibility by land. They'd swim, dig for clams if the tide was right, and eat, sometimes not returning until dusk. The unadulterated joy of those two summers between childhood and young adulthood was untouchable, sacred for its innocence—

Caro opened her eyes. Covering them with her hand she sat up and put on her sunglasses. The twosome came immediately into sight.

"Livia, look this way." Nina directed her niece toward an invisible spot to the right of the lens. "That's great," she said. Crouching around her niece, she clicked multiple shots.

Livia sidestepped the eye of the lens and held up her hand to beg no more.

Nina let the camera drop onto her chest. "No, Livia. I'm not done yet. The light is perfect."

Livia gripped her aunt's arm with both hands. "Please, we've done enough."

"No. Now get in place again." Nina jerked her arm free.

Livia planted her feet and stared at the spot on the ground where her aunt indicated. Slim and flat-chested, Livia didn't have the full-fledged figure of other girls her age. She was all young ballerina arms and legs but without the apparent grace that either training or maturity brings. And so she stood in coltish stubbornness until the sea coughed up a light spray, inducing her to move. She raised her foot to take up her position, but stopped mid-air.

"Get," Nina ordered.

Livia stumbled into place and tears seeped out from under her lowered eyelids.

Caro watched the scene play out between aunt and niece, photographer and model. She wished she could see Livia's face to know what made her such a special subject, for even the perspective from her back stirred Caro. There was something about the way Livia's plaited hair purled along her spine, wavelike—a symbolic tribute to the ocean that rushed homeward in dedicated routine only to leave with equal constancy. Or was the tidal movement a metaphor for the girl's position on the threshold of young adulthood, her defense mechanism against the uncertainties of life?

Nina observed Livia's slackness through the lens. "Shit!" she said half aloud, and then to Livia, "All right. Get out of here."

Livia started toward her aunt but when she spotted Caro she set off for home, making a wide arc well out of reach of the approaching woman.

Nina put up her hands. "I told you she's shy."

Caro shrugged off the apologetic words. "She's young," she said and joined Nina as she followed Livia's retreat.

Livia pumped her arms as she ran and her honey-blonde braid bumped lightly on her back. When she got to the catwalk, she skidded to a stop.

Caro hoped she would turn around. She waited for it without knowing why. But Livia did not oblige and disappeared from sight.

Nina replaced her camera in its case and then put the case into a large, plastic-lined canvas bag safe from the elements. "I'm anal," she said, patting the bag.

Caro lowered herself onto the chair. Nina leaned back on her elbows on the blanket and stretched out her legs, crossing them at the ankles.

Caro noticed Nina's smoothly waxed skin and immaculate pedicure. If Marcie had been here, she would've already made appointments for them at Tommy's spa. On her own, Caro was lazy about her grooming, then felt embarrassed when she found herself in a situation like this one. She desperately tried to hide her chipped red toenails. She gave a small toss of her head.

"Does Livia model for you a lot?"

"Bribery used to work. Lately, it's only on command. She has no idea what a rare beauty she is. Just heats up the camera."

"How long is she staying with you?"

"Two months. Maybe more. Her mother and new husband are traveling through Singapore and China, part honeymoon, part business. He's an exporter looking to find a base in Hong Kong." Nina smirked. "The family thought my being in the arts—a photographer—was capricious and more prone to multiple divorces. Meanwhile Tommy and I have been together eighteen years. This is Carmen's third husband."

"Where's her dad?" Caro asked.

"Oscar's sweet and stays as involved as he can in Livia's life, but he's busy with his own family. Inherited a handful when he remarried—three teenage stepsons."

Nina raised herself into a sitting position and, gathering her hair in a thick tail, flipped it to one side. She shifted the talk to Caro. "Gwen mentioned you were supposed to rent with someone else. Did she change her plans?"

Caro hesitated. "She died."

"Oh, I'm sorry. I shouldn't be so nosy."

"It's fine. It's just that I knew Marcie for a long time. We were, I mean, she *was* an incredible person." Caro said.

"Do you have family," Nina asked.

"My daughter, Abby, lives in London. And my husband's been dead for several years, so I'm used to doing things on my own."

Caro felt a current of unease slither along her backbone. She was uncomfortable talking about people she loved to someone she had met only the night before, no matter how genuine Nina seemed.

"If we can do anything at all..." Nina offered.

"What?" Caro asked.

"...you know, with Marcie not here."

"Thanks," Caro said. And then, "I think I'll head in."

They got up simultaneously; Caro helped gather Nina's belongings.

When they got to the steps that climbed up the dune, Caro saw Livia at the window in the tower. In the bright sunlight, the girl appeared made out of gold. Caro suddenly felt her heart pound, and an inexplicable desire to get to know Livia rose to her consciousness.

Nina tapped Caro on the shoulder.

"Sorry," Caro said startled, and turned quickly away.

"No problem. You can put everything down here," Nina said.

Caro set down a large canvas bag and a retractable tripod. When she straightened up, she couldn't help herself and glanced in the direction of the tower. Livia was gone.

"Thanks for the extra arms." Nina pushed through the double doors and called, "Hey, I'm home," to her niece.

Later that evening, inspired by Livia's surprising entry into her life and Nina's own attractiveness, Caro pondered again the connection between ideal love and beauty. As for herself, she didn't look in a mirror unless the task called for it: fixing her hair or applying makeup. Even in public bathrooms where rows of glass striped the walls above the sinks, Caro shrunk from her reflection.

She wasn't ugly, just not pretty. An artist friend once told her she was a study in lightness. Oatmeal and bone and sand came to mind when she contemplated her features. The irises of her eyes were small and of the palest river-stone grey. Habitual scowling had driven a rut between her eyes, which she obsessively tried to rub smooth with her forefinger. Everything about her was millimeters out of balance. Even her right eyebrow arched higher than the left, a defect made obvious when she wore her glasses and one brow dipped below the frame.

Caro let out a small sigh. In the Hamptons all the women seemed bred from a common pool of superior genes. Not knowing any of them personally made them easier to ignore as they passed her on the sidewalk. In contrast, Nina's close proximity and friendly personality were going to make it impossible for Caro to forget her own physical failings.

Snickering at herself, she flicked off the bathroom light and went into the bedroom where she'd left her pen and journal on the dresser. The pen, unlike the mirror, seemed forgiving. If there was any reflection to be had from the pen, it was of her soul.

As always when the mirror disappointed, she felt all the more inspired to create. Images transformed into words that swam in and out of her awareness. She wanted to hook the words in her handwriting, to feel the physical sense of each curve and curl stringing the letters together in a cursive mosaic. The transference of inspiration to the pen and then onto the page was a choreography of sorts; the only guesswork was in the mechanics of style.

Caro opened a spiral notebook—its pages clean and tight—and positioned a new pen, only to have the words, that moments before had been poised for expression, drift away. An unstoppable stream of snapshots of Livia filtered into her consciousness. Caro studied every image, holding each one up to a mental frame as if someone was passing her tangible photographs. And once again, she felt an unnamable attraction to the girl.

Writing, I think, is not apart from living. Writing is a kind of double living. The writer experiences everything twice. Once in reality and once in that mirror which waits always before or behind.

~CATHERINE DRINKER BOWEN

CHAPTER FIVE

Caro negotiated her way through half-naked, oil-slick bodies in order to get closer to the water. Now mid-afternoon, the temperature hovered at seventy-eight, and a northeasterly breeze kicked up the surf.

The day before, she'd bought a portable beach canopy and already acknowledged the value of her purchase as she sat in the shelter of its nylon walls, immune to wind, sun, and prying eyes. She'd eaten lunch in clean comfort and now, with her skin a pale pink from an hour of sunning, she was enjoying a brief respite when she heard someone talking.

"Aunt Nina says you're a poet."

As the words registered, Caro's heart sped up and her eyes came open with a start. As each inch of Livia came into Caro's view, she expelled her breath in a soft rush, unaware she'd been holding a lungful of air in her chest. She'd been wrong.

Her earlier imaginings about what Livia looked like close up did not compare with the beauty that stood before her.

Yet, it wasn't only the sea-foam eyes or the straight nose or the rose lips set in a firm chin that made Caro pale from the sheer amazement of Livia's prettiness. Nor was it her freshly tanned skin. It was Livia's expression; she owned a poise in spite of the way she chewed at her lower lip. Caro couldn't bear to dwell on her any longer. Poem or picture—Livia could raise either to life!

"Yes, I am," Caro said. She adjusted herself and gestured for Livia to join her under the cover of the canopy. "Do you like poetry?"

Livia nodded, and then sat cross-legged at Caro's feet.

"So where's home, Livia?"

"It used to be Westchester, but I don't know where after the summer," Livia said.

"Oh, why is that?" Caro asked.

"Mom and my new step-dad have to figure that out depending on where he opens up his business. Right now they're in Thailand."

"Thailand...that would be a big change," Caro said.

Livia looked away toward the ocean.

Caro held up a bottle of iced green tea from the cooler. "It's all I have."

Livia accepted the drink. "Are you here just for the summer too?"

"Yes," Caro said. "Reminds me of when I was just a little older than you and I used to come and stay with my sister and her husband."

"Are they still here?"

"Not anymore, but I remember the fun we used to have," Caro said.

"Like what?"

"Clamming was one of my favorite things."

Livia's eyes brightened. "Me, too! Uncle Tommy and I go so much Aunt Nina is sick of clams. She says she's running out of recipes."

"I love them cold on the half-shell," Caro said.

"Maybe you can come with us one time."

"I'd like that." After Nina and Tommy had warned Caro of Livia's shyness, she was glad how open she was. "So tell me more about your interest in poetry."

"I'm a poet, too."

"How wonderful! What do you write about?"

"Different things," Livia said.

"Like what," Caro asked.

"Stuff," Livia said curtly.

"Nothing you can share?"

"Not today."

"Another time, maybe," Caro said.

Livia handed Caro the half-empty bottle. "I've gotta go."

"You'll come back," Caro urged, inching forward with each word so that by the time Livia was standing outside the cabana, Caro's chin jutted out of the opening.

Livia glanced over her shoulder, shrugged, and then took off through the human netting of beach-goers who had settled to within a couple of yards of her tent.

Caro dropped back onto the squat canvas seat. "Well, I'll be," she muttered, and wondered what caused Livia's sudden turn-a-round in her mood. Did she bore the girl or maybe she expected too much from her? Thinking back to herself at that age, Caro remembered she'd kept her writing private.

She smiled to herself, and wondered what else she might have had in common with Livia at twelve years old. Caro recalled one time slinking out of the local record store with Beethoven's Ninth Symphony in a brown bag. She made it home without meeting any of her friends, but upon opening the back door, her younger sister, Rose, ambushed her.

Pulling the record from its paper sleeve she flapped it in the air and scuttled into the kitchen where Tereza was helping their mother prepare supper.

"Looky, looky," Rose sniggered and brandished the record under Caro's nose. "You're such a weirdo. Everyone at school thinks so."

Caro lunged for the record and missed.

Rose pranced around the kitchen.

"You're such a dork," Tereza said to Rose. "When are you going to act like a *normal* person?" She shook her head in condemnation, then resumed setting the table.

Caro's mother split her loyalty depending on the kind of day she had at work: on occasion she defended Caro; other times, she took her frustrations out on her middle child, about whom she once remarked that her odd features and pleading mouth reminded her of the guppies in the fish bowl next to her daughter's bed.

That evening, her mother shook her ladle at Rose in disapproval. "Give the record back right now," she ordered.

"Here," Rose said, and flung the disc in Caro's direction.

The record slid passed Caro on the linoleum floor. Stumbling to retrieve it, Caro mis-stepped and the record cracked under the weight of her heel. "Look what you made me do," she screeched. "That was all the money I had."

"Sor-ry," Rose said, jutting her chin out at Caro.

"No you're not. You're happy it broke," Caro yelled.

"Shut up, Caro," her mother warned. "Rose said she was sorry. I'm sick of the two of you always bickering. Just shut up. You're giving me a headache."

"No! I saved for three months, and now I have nothing. Make her pay for it!"

Her mother stomped across the room to Caro. "I'm not warning you again."

Caro grabbed the wooden spoon from her mother and dropping onto the floor, she began smashing the cracked record. "I hate you," she screamed. "I hate all of you."

Caro had been in the house for about an hour, potting a basil plant when Livia climbed the steps to the deck and hesitantly held out a sheet of paper. "Here."

Caro saw in the nervous lines around Livia's mouth how difficult it was for her to have come. She accepted the proffered poem. "Sit over there if you want."

Livia sat on her hands on the edge of the divan.

The script was clean for a pre-teen, and bold enough that Caro didn't need her glasses. "Clock Shop," she read and began to recite:

Time is harsh outside the walls of the clock shop
where the occasional passerby takes out her watch to see
where she has to be, reminding me of my mother
looking at her watch in some foreign city far away from me.

Centuries of history reign inside the clock shop where chimes
and gongs keep track of time like a fisherman trawling for his catch,
too busy to take notice of the minutes passing or the correct time
and no one takes out their watch because clocks are all around you.

In a world where time can be an enemy and where the hour
is often spent waiting for a woman to check her watch
I embrace time when I am in the clock shop.

Livia didn't wait for Caro's response. She asked, "Do you believe in wishes coming true?"

"I do. I know they don't come true all the time, but I believe in the power of thoughts to turn wishes into realities."

"Even if they seem impossible?"

"That just means having stronger faith." Caro noticed that Livia was staring at the tower of her aunt's house. "I noticed you spend a lot of time up there."

"I feel like I can see to the other side of the ocean. Uncle Tommy said he's seen sharks and dolphins with his telescope."

"Have you seen anything yet?"

"Not much, but he said I will as long as I'm patient." Livia puffed up her mouth and blew out a stream of air; she seemed to deflate.

"It's hard to be patient though, isn't it?" Caro remarked.

Livia gave a slow nod.

"Livia, there you are. I kind of thought so." Nina rounded the corner of the catwalk and joined them. She said to Caro, "I told you she was shy and now it turns out that she likes coming over. I didn't fully realize what I was doing when I told her you were a poet."

"I'm happy you did. I enjoy her company." Caro folded Livia's poem in quarters and tucked it under her coaster, hidden from Nina's view.

Nina cupped Livia's chin. "I need for her to realize that photography is as important to me as poetry is to her."

"I do," Livia said. "I just don't like to pose for *your* art."

"Anyway," Nina clucked in dismissal. "And how are you faring," she asked Caro.

"Better than I thought I would. It's been so many years since I vacationed for any length of time. So having you and Tommy and Livia next door is turning out to be really nice."

"Then I know you'll feel free to come knocking any time. In fact, come for breakfast tomorrow about ten. Sundays at our house are long and leisurely and I make a bakery or crepe surprise. Right, kiddo?"

Livia gave a quick toss of her head.

"Sounds delicious," Caro said.

Standing behind Livia, Nina pulled the length of her niece's braid through her hand. "In the meantime, Tommy is waiting for his girls, so we need to leave."

Livia sucked in her bottom lip as she peered at Caro and then at her poem.

Caro patted the coaster, indicating its safekeeping.

Later, with thoughts of Livia still alive, Caro booted up her computer. Her gaze fixed on a spider building a web in the corner of the ceiling. She studied the miniscule black body releasing centimeters of thread for its design until her focus dissipated and she stepped into the obscure world of creation.

Fantasy liberated Caro from the constraints and rigors of reality. It was where she was her most uncensored self, a place she disappeared to almost daily, if even for seconds. It was where the stuff of her poetry came from.

She began to type—a halting cadence of her fingers on the keyboard.

A golden twist of nouns and verbs
in mute and mock display
with flying curls of
metaphors in costumed disarray.

A buried mix of hidden rhymes
so seldom sought to hear...

Caro waited for further inspiration in stillness, her fingers resting in place on the keys. She typed and deleted several times, all false starts. An hour later, after numerous permutations she began to grumble. "Hear *what?*" She sucked in her breath and stared at the emerging poem for several minutes as a dread rose from her belly.

No matter how many poems she'd written, beginning a new work produced such fear that the taste in her mouth made her throat close. And it was only with great effort she reassured herself that after the piece settled for a day or so she'd add and revise until the flow and melody of the words revealed the truths she intended.

Caro believed that writing in any genre was an exercise in excavating truths, so she tried always to go inward as far as she could. For example, she used to write poems about Abby during her growing-up years. But once Abby was in high school, trying to find the truth about their relationship became increasingly difficult as her daughter began to distance herself from Caro emotionally, talking more to Zach than to her.

Caro thought it was a developmental stage Abby was going through and so she gave her daughter space. In retrospect, Caro concluded that Abby took her mother's silence as not caring because by the time Abby entered college she confided almost exclusively in Zach. The few times Caro tried to talk to Abby, her daughter's standard reply was, "Thanks anyway, Mom. Dad has it covered," or for topics about the men in her life, it was "My friends understand better."

Caro could not—dare not—define what her relationship was with Livia. Did she now even utter the word, *love*, aloud? Even as she repeated it to herself, the notion of loving Livia both frightened and excited her.

Platonic love was not, as Caro previously understood, confined to its contemplative aspects of beauty and knowledge. Rather, homosexual relations were acknowledged as long as the coming together helped to produce greater virtue in each partner. A way, Caro thought sardonically—just as today—of making same-sex love morally digestible.

When I look on you a moment, then I can speak no more, but my tongue falls silent, and at once a delicate flame courses beneath my skin, and with my eyes I see nothing, and my ears hum, and a wet sweat bathes me, and a trembling seizes me all over.

~SAPPHO

CHAPTER SIX

Caro exited Westhampton Bakery holding a large cappuccino. She had her sights on a vacant bench and hurried toward it, keeping watch for anyone ready to challenge her. The town was always full of activity at mid-afternoon, when the bathers and sated sun-worshippers cruised the shops along Main Street.

Caro typically avoided the crowds but after happening upon a letter from Marcie that she'd found inside the cover of her planner, she found the bungalow too quiet, and drove to town.

She was just sitting down outside the bakery when—

"Caro!"

Caro's head snapped in the direction of the voice at the same moment she heard the automatic clicking of a camera shutter. Instinctively covering her face, she jerked her hand upward and coffee spilled, splattering on to her pants. "What are you *doing*?"

Nina lowered the camera. "Thought you might like to have a souvenir."

Caro flicked the dripping liquid from her fingers. "Don't do that again."

Nina handed her a rumpled wad of tissues. "Sorry."

Caro blotted the wet spots. "I don't like having my picture taken."

A few awkward moments passed. "Can I buy you another?" Nina offered.

Caro unclenched her jaw. "This one's fine."

It was only when they sat that Caro saw Livia on the other side of the street in front of the confectionary. A boy came out carrying two ice cream cones and handed one to her.

"Tommy's nephew, Alex," Nina explained. "He's like her big brother."

Caro crossed her legs in an attempt at a casual posture even though her stomach twittered with delight at Livia's presence. "Is he from around here?"

"About thirty minutes west, near Bayport."

Livia reared her head back in laughter as Alex jerked on her braid. She punched him playfully on the arm when he pulled her hair a second time.

"It worries me how immature she is," Nina confided. "She's going into high school in September and the kids are going to tear her apart. Almost fourteen and she acts like someone half her age."

Caro kept quiet. To her, Livia's naiveté elevated her beauty and made her worthy of deeper introspection, and Caro would resent any alterations that would modify her behavior or appearance.

"Not too long ago I tried saying something, but the idea of makeup, hard rock, and boys has absolutely no attraction for her." Nina's words came out like a lament. And then out of frustration she uttered, "Sometimes I feel like yelling at her to wake up!"

"On the contrary, I sympathize with her because I was the same way," Caro said. "I never felt that I fit in as a teenager."

"When did you start becoming interested in boys?"

"I wouldn't dare tell you that, you'd laugh. But I was... older."

Nina grimaced and shook her head.

Caro pondered how Livia shouldn't have to be made to grow up before she was ready. Nina was an artist. Why couldn't she recognize the rarity of Livia's innocence and her potential to develop intellectually and creatively?

Livia propped her feet against the base of a parking meter, and with one hand secured on the coin deposit and her body tilted outward, swung around the pole. Her madras blouse and pony tail held high in a bright red scrunchie reflected her youthful character.

"Was Abby a late bloomer?" Nina asked.

Caro shook her head emphatically. "She matured very early and liked all the supposedly *normal* teen things..." Caro noticed Nina scowl as she turned her camera over in her hands.

Nina gave a small sigh and gazed across the street at Livia. "Do you think Abby would have liked posing for me?"

"Audiences of any kind or number exhilarate her. And she inherited her father's magnetic presence, the kind that prompted people to look around when he walked into a room even though he was quite ordinary looking."

"Wouldn't it have been nice then if Abby was my niece and Livia your daughter?"

Caro's immediate reaction was to say, Very nice indeed. She didn't know Livia well enough to know for sure, but so far Livia was easy to be with, expected little in the way of entertainment, and wanted nothing more than an attentive ear to her verse, unlike Caro's daughter, who navigated life blinkered and unbending. Nevertheless, wasn't it wrong for a mother to want to trade off her daughter for another more genial model? To Nina she said, "I think Abby would like you a lot."

"Do you get over to London often to see her?" Nina asked.

"Time has a way of flying by," Caro said. She was embarrassed to admit that in the year and a half Abby had lived in London, she had yet to visit. She kept telling herself she loved her daughter—it was just such hard work being with her. Abby was her daddy's girl, and it seemed that the only common thing they had in common was their DNA.

"Isn't that the truth," Nina said. "With myself I can hardly believe where the years went. I'm going to be forty-three next birthday and my accomplishments are a husband and a house in the Hamptons."

"You sound disappointed," Caro said.

Nina was about to reply when Tommy jogged across the street toward them with Livia and Alex tagging behind.

"How about an early supper and a movie tonight? *Harry Potter* for us," Tommy said, indicating Livia and Alex along with himself. "*Julie and Julia* for you two?"

"Caro?" Nina asked.

"Sounds great," Caro said and tugged lightly at Livia's braid.

Caro mounted her bike on her car and went next door.

Livia was sitting on the porch steps, her face smothered in her palms. The twin tufts of baby-fine hair that were her eyebrows rose above her fingertips at Caro's unexpected appearance.

"Hello." Caro noticed a faint crease across the bridge of Livia's nose, the beginning of a glower behind her hands.

When Livia didn't respond, Caro sat down next to her. "You've got quite a frown for such a beautiful, sunny day."

"So..."

"*So* what's wrong?" Caro asked.

"I'm lonely. And I'm bored, that's what's wrong."

"We can do things together," Caro blurted. "That's why I came over today."

"It's different. Aunt Nina understands. She felt really bad," Livia said.

"About what?"

"About that my cousin had to cancel her visit because she got mono and has to stay in for six weeks. That's half the summer!"

"How long was she planning to stay?" Caro asked.

"Two weeks. We get together every summer. Either I go to her house in Maryland or she comes to me. This year she was coming here to be at the beach."

Two weeks without Livia alone! Caro exhaled in relief. "I think what I planned for us today is especially, exactly what you need now."

Caro saw a subtle rise in Livia's expression. "Your aunt told me you like to bird-watch so I thought we'd go over to Shelter Island. Interested?"

"I guess," Livia said, and took off to look for her aunt.

Caro and Livia boarded the ferry at Sag Harbor for the ten-minute ride across Noyack Bay, one of three deep harbors along the twenty-five-mile coastline. An eight-thousand acre windswept island town tucked between the twin forks of eastern Long Island—the rural northern fork with its horse farms and apple orchards and its posh southern counterpart, the Hamptons—Shelter Island was known for its mist-laden bluffs, vast tracts of salt marsh, and pebbled beaches.

As they drove off the ferry, Caro headed toward the Visitors Center at the Mashomack Preserve, which was to be their starting point. "I went online and downloaded the bird-watching trails. But I thought you might want to first bike along the coast and check out the boats in the marinas. Your Aunt Nina said—"

Livia interrupted. "You talk a lot to Aunt Nina."

"Guess I do. Is that a bad thing?"

Livia shrugged and focused on unfastening her bike from the trunk rack.

Before long, Caro's car was left in the distance as they pedaled toward Coecles Inlet on North Ferry Road. She'd estimated the nine-mile ride to take about an hour, given the hilly terrain, and praised herself for having stayed in shape over the years. In the city she bicycled often. It was so much easier than hailing a taxi or fighting the elbowing throngs in the subways.

They rode in silence with Livia in the lead. The fat tires of her mountain bike dispersed gravel in wavy rivulets as she swerved from side to side, keeping time to some inner rhythm.

Before long, she spotted a female osprey who had built her nest on the top mast of a dry-docked schooner. "Look!" Livia pointed and sped up for about fifty yards before turning into the driveway of Gates Marina. She jumped off her bike under the nest. When Caro caught up, Livia exclaimed, "She's so huge! Awesome, right?"

"Awesome," Caro mimicked. "I never saw one this close up before."

"Know what the coolest thing about them is?"

"What?"

"They can make the toes on their talons go backward or forward depending on the prey they're trying to catch. Like this." She demonstrated with her fingers.

"I think this one is scary-looking with its beady eyes. And its beak looks like it could tear into anything."

"That's because they're related to the hawk...very protective of their nests. Watch how it tracks my every move." Livia made a slow rotation around the schooner.

"You sound quite the expert."

"Uncle Tommy taught me. He's the one that got me interested in this stuff."

Caro followed Livia's lead around the nest. The gawking of the predator chilled Caro. She felt as if it intuited her own ravenous attraction toward Livia. Afraid, Caro withdrew.

Livia tugged at Caro's arm.

The girl's touch startled Caro and she was rocketed back in time to when her daughter used to get her attention in the same way. Sometimes when Caro didn't want to be bothered she'd yank her hand out of Abby's reach. With Livia, she welcomed the girl's touch and so she relaxed her hand. "What?"

"We have to move away so she'll feel safe enough to leave her nest. Then we can watch her take flight."

"All right." Caro followed Livia to the road, where they waited behind the massive trunk of an old sycamore.

Within a minute the osprey gave the area one last inspection and then pushed off her perch. Her long body arched and executed a deep dive. As it neared water level it pushed upward and settled into a slow, steady wingbeat.

Livia sensed Caro's reaction and turned to her. "I told you it would be awesome."

"It definitely was," Caro said.

The girl's broad smile was a wreath around her face. After the shared moment with the osprey, she loosened up. By the time they got to Coecles Harbor Livia claimed hunger and thirst with unguarded exuberance.

"You seem to get along really well with your uncle," Caro said over a platter of fried clams and chips.

"Yeah, he's great. Aunt Nina, too, when she doesn't have her camera. Last spring they took me to Maine for a birding festival. Was great fun!"

"I don't know about birds. Is there a special species that you like better than most?"

"Sea birds. The ospreys are cool because they're predators and supposedly big, tough guys, but all they hunt is fish."

"Fish aren't sacred?" Caro asked only half seriously.

"Nah, just boring." Livia munched on french fries and then almost as an afterthought she added, "Plus you can spot the osprey without using binoculars."

"I'd think you'd want to see them up close," Caro commented.

Livia shook her head, and then swung her leg around over the bench and chucked her half-eaten food in the trash barrel. She sat down again, but this time with her back to the picnic table, and made noises through her straw in the soda.

Livia's body language made Caro wonder if the girl felt the camera lens to be as invasive as being objectified by the binoculars? Caro pressed the issue. "But you like using your uncle's telescope and that zooms objects in."

Livia didn't answer.

Caro attempted a matter-of-fact tone. "In poetry, details make the poems work. Elizabeth Bishop was famous for her eye for detail. She believed it was a poet's task to examine things at close range. In one of her poems, she wrote, '... from the window I see an immense city, carefully revealed, made delicate by overworkmanship, detail upon detail, cornice upon façade.'"

Livia appeared unresponsive, but Caro knew differently by the discernible tilt of her ward's profile in her direction. "She's talking about love. We know that from the title. Love enabled the lover to make even a big city delicate because of the details. If you're going to be a poet, Livia, you're going to be under scrutiny. Just like being viewed from behind binoculars, or a camera lens."

Livia glared at Caro over her shoulder.

Caro held the youngster's stare with equal resolve, until without warning, Livia's face dissolved into tears.

Caro pushed up from the bench and reached out to her.

Sniffling and swiping at her nose, Livia rejected the gesture and sprinted to her bike. With one foot on the pedal ready to take off, she asked in a choked voice, "Can we go now?"

Caro nodded, then watched Livia wheel down the road and around a bend before coming to a stop behind a grove of white birch. She hadn't meant to get so serious on their inaugural jaunt and castigated herself for frightening Livia away. She could see the girl through the netting of leaves and tree branches, an incomplete puzzle—the tail of a beribboned braid, the corner of a scraped elbow, sections of a shin and a forearm, the sock-covered turn of an ankle.

Caro couldn't clearly make out the pieces of Livia's face. Were the green eyes turned to sharp slivers the same way Caro's had when first introduced to the notion of scrutiny?

As a child-poet, Livia had to learn the importance of play. Her poetry had suffered in her early years because of a rigid upbringing where laughter was the odd surprise, as rare an occurrence as someone knocking at her family's door on a neighborly whim. Indeed, even as a young adult, Caro wondered about the success of her father's business, given his somber personality.

Not until Zach did she experience her first full belly laugh. Or view her writing with any sense of humor. She'd believed that serious poetry warranted solemnity both in mood and language. As it turned out, in later years she drew from the absurdities in life for some of her most important work.

So, yes! Today was reserved for fun. Caro approached Livia, dangling in front of her the bright green stem of a gladiola to which clung a furry yellow caterpillar. "Think he'll want to tag along for a boat ride?"

Livia screwed up her face. "That? It's a dumb insect."

Caro twisted the stem for Livia to get a better look. "Technically, it's in the larval form of the moth family. It's not considered an insect until its metamorphosis into a butterfly."

"I know they turn into butterflies," Livia said churlishly, and then in a more civil tone asked, "What's the word you used?"

"Metamorphosis. Means transformation. An example every child knows as the ugly duckling that becomes the swan, or the frog that turns into the handsome prince."

Livia grinned. "A handsome prince? In that case," she said and entwined the end of the stem in the metal prongs of the basket on her handle bars. "Hang on," she called to her passenger and they took off for the harbor.

After that, Caro made sure to keep the conversation light and consequently, Livia's mood remained buoyant for the rest of the excursion. They returned to Westhampton at dusk, and Caro noted with pleasure the enthusiasm with which Livia recounted their day to her aunt and uncle.

After a supper of cold chicken and a salad, Caro took her coffee out to the deck to enjoy under the full moon. The heady aromas of wild rosemary and thyme merged with those of the basil and lavender she'd potted. Their distinctive fragrances resurrected memories of Zach and Marcie cooking one of their Saturday-night gourmet specials for Caro.

Zach had begun the tradition with Abby. When their daughter moved to Boston for graduate school, he had been excited to discover Marcie's culinary skills and together they had prepared meals that were artful both in presentation and taste.

Suddenly Nina's voice rang out, eclipsing Caro's peace and quiet. Both Caro's and the Winters' houses sat on narrow, pie-shaped slices of land with decks that were side-by-side with only an alley the width of a city sidewalk bridging the distance. Thus, it wasn't unusual to overhear fragments of conversation when the breezes were swirling in the right direction. Twice Nina had even called over and invited Caro to join her and Tommy for a nightcap, knowing she was within earshot.

Tonight no wind was necessary to hear Nina's loud retort to her husband. "It's not your decision if I publish them."

Caro flipped onto her side on the chaise lounge. In the brightness of patio lamps she spied Tommy pacing in front of Nina, who was sitting in a dining chair.

"I won't allow you to exploit her," he was saying. "In spite of what you may think, I have a say in this matter. She's my niece, too."

"Technically she's not," Nina retorted.

"*Technically* she's still a child."

Caro's heart kicked in her chest, knowing they were discussing Livia.

"How should I have dressed her? In a goddamn flannel nightgown?" Nina was screeching. "She was in a cotton slip."

"Stop shouting at me," Tommy warned. "It's the poses. The facial expressions. They're wrong for someone her age."

"That's what critics said about Sally Mann's work of her children and she turned out to be one of the top female photographers of the century," Nina said.

Tommy grabbed the arms of his wife's chair and leaned in close to her. "So this is what the photographs are all about—angling for a controversy that might jump-start your career."

Nina's posture stiffened, her mouth a drawn, thin line across her face.

"Resonates, doesn't it, Nina? If so, use any rationale you want, you're still dead wrong."

When Nina didn't speak, Tommy yelled, "Fuck! You're stubborn!" Turning on his heel, he started for the house.

When Nina also stormed inside and their deck lights went out, Caro sat up. She mentally replayed what she'd overheard to try and figure out exactly what they were arguing about. Photographs of Livia obviously, but disagreeing about what she was wearing...her poses. Tommy was furious over the pictures, but how bad could they really be?

Caro ran inside to her computer and typed in Sally Mann's name in the Google search bar.

Apparently, Mann became an overnight success in the early 1990s with her collection of black and white photographs of her three children, all under the age of ten. The pictures, taken at the family's summer cabin, explored typical childhood themes such as dressing up and playing board games. Others, however, touched on darker themes of injury, sexuality, and death.

Caro read that the controversy over the collection included accusations of child pornography. One nude image in particular of Mann's four-year-old daughter was banned in certain publications because it displayed the child's nipples and vagina.

Caro's breaths came in short bursts while she tried to conjure what kind of photos Nina had taken of Livia. She stared into space, attempting to retrieve Tommy's words to his wife. He hadn't said anything of nude images. Of that, Caro was certain. She would have remembered that; Caro couldn't even begin to contemplate strangers viewing Livia nude!

Her own obsession with the girl produced another kind of inner explosion. Vague imaginings of Livia half-dressed in seductive poses caused a shudder that purled along her spine to the pit of her belly. Caro dwelled in her thoughts for moments longer than she wanted. Yet, she was helpless to pull away until guilt overcame her and she ran outside and onto the beach. She didn't stop running until she was ankle-deep in the cold, midnight surf.

One should really use the camera as though tomorrow you'd be stricken blind.

~DOROTHEA LANGE

CHAPTER SEVEN

Caro peered out at the rain, the kind of steady stream that showed no sign of letting up. She had awakened to the spattering on the roof during the night, then heard an irritating plunk on the tiles in the bedroom hallway. Gwen had forgotten to mention a leak. By morning, the pail Caro had put in place was a quarter full.

The grim grayness that accompanied the wet weather also produced an indolence in her that she couldn't shake. Instead of working she ate snacks and watched TV until late afternoon, when she finally sat down to write.

Because it was smaller than the other bedrooms, Caro preferred the intimacy of her space in the guest room. Gwen had covered the walls with fabric of dark carmine, and hung matching triple panels on the windows. Caro felt cushioned by the heavy décor, hidden to the point of invisibility. Covered windows and no mirrors—she'd stored the dresser mirror in the closet. Nothing in the room reflected her image.

She picked up her favorite pen, a Montblanc fountain pen, whose design honored Virginia Woolf. Whenever Caro held this pen she was brought back to her initial encounter with the author.

Before Caro studied Woolf, she had subscribed to the notion that Zach, as her husband and, at the time, the main breadwinner of the family, deserved a study in the main part of their house. She'd set up a makeshift office in the basement next to the exercise equipment. But once Caro embraced Woolf's sentiments regarding the importance of women writers, she and Zach had numerous arguments about her new priorities.

As her determination intensified, his refusal to give in progressed from polite denial to outright forbiddance. But she'd stood fast, and for a few years they were at loggerheads. Strangely, this was the only point of difference Zach ever had regarding her career. And it was one of most importance to Caro.

The sale of her first book finally forced him into accepting her right to have her own room to work in. When they built their last home, her study was on the third floor overlooking the Hudson River.

How would Woolf have advised Livia? Ignore the pressure of peers. Forget worrying about wearing the right shade of lipstick or the trendiest jeans, the author might have said. If there was to be any concern, it should be bolstering Livia's already burgeoning sensitivity to life's ordinary miracles.

Caro copied out what she had of the unfinished poem she'd begun for Livia; she added the title as well as the final lines of the second stanza.

The Yellow Braid
A golden twist of nouns and verbs
in mute and mock display
with flying curls of
metaphors in costumed disarray.

A buried mix of hidden rhymes
so seldom sought to hear
a drawstring bag of adjectives
so difficult to bear.

A solitary arc of sunlight crossed Caro's desk and she opened up the French doors. The rain had diminished to a mist; she spotted a rainbow in the western sky. It was a sign she thought, a sanctioning of her thoughts.

Then a figure in a navy slicker intersected her line of vision. Livia lifted her face, causing her hood to fall away.

Waving, Caro jogged down the catwalk and called out Livia's name. "Hey, come on up for awhile."

"I can't. Aunt Nina's going to show me how to make fudge." Livia spoke to Caro from the bottom of the steps that led up from the beach.

After a lopsided life of ignoring her family and friends for her poetry, it was, ironically, a younger version of herself who was reeling her back in toward her center at the same time that Livia was driving Caro to the edges of reason.

❧

The next day was sunny. The sky appeared sharper and brighter, as if a person was experiencing it from an elevated place of consciousness. Caro put on shorts and was just about to head out to the deck when she heard someone knocking.

It was the chauffeur she'd seen waxing the Bentley owned by the people who lived in the mansion that faced Dune Road. "Can I help you?" she said.

"I'm Jimmy. Mrs. Tyler sent this." He handed Caro an envelope.

Caro fingered it and was about to thank him and close the door when he said, "She wants me to return with a reply. Said to tell you she didn't know there was a celebrity in her backyard." He tilted his head and peered at her from an odd angle, apparently trying to see if he recognized her from television. "Are you really a celebrity?"

His sincerity drew out her lips in a smile. "A minnow in a sea of whales, Jimmy." She extracted a hand-written invitation from its linen paper envelope. It was for a supper in her honor. Mrs. Tyler noted she'd read all of Caro's poetry and could hardly wait to meet her in person. She'd have each of her books open and waiting for a personal autograph.

Caro hesitated. She would like to have asked Nina about Mrs. Tyler before giving her answer. But she didn't want to risk being rude to someone who appreciated her work. Anyway, it was only one supper. "Tell her, thanks. I look forward to meeting her as well."

After Jimmy left, Caro trudged next door over the dunes to talk to Nina. She found her wearing her apron and holding a whisk.

Caro lifted a mug from its chrome hook and held it out for Nina to fill. "Got a batch of chocolate chunk to put in for Tommy and then I'm done."

"What do you know about the Tylers?" Caro asked.

Nina folded the chocolate into the batter, offering the spoon to Caro for a lick. "You got the invitation, huh? Are you going?"

"Hard to say no when I'm the star guest. I was just wondering what I was getting myself into."

"It'll be a superlative gig," Nina said. "Phyllis Tyler doesn't do anything half-assed. She's a patron of the arts. Donated the bulk of the money to restore the library."

"Do you know her well?"

"Tommy more than me. Both families bought in Westhampton long before it became chic so they've known each other for eons. Aside from that, she's one of his favorite clients. Very down to earth. Soft-spoken and easy to please. A real lady and not at all the Hampton socialite type. You'll love her."

"Sounds great then, as long as you and Tommy are going." Caro peeked into the family and living rooms. "Where is he anyway?"

Nina banged the whisk against the rim of the copper bowl. "Out."

"And Livia?"

A wave of angry disdain transformed Nina's calm exterior. "With him. He thinks I'm perverting her." With that she stomped into her office and came out waving a photo mailer. "Look at these and tell me what *you* think."

Caro withdrew and raised her hands, refusing to take them. "I'm the wrong one to ask."

Nina shoved the mailer at Caro's chest. "You're an intelligent person with a PhD. A mother, for God's sake, with opinions. All I want is an objective opinion."

Caro slid the photographs from the cardboard sleeve. Afraid of what she was going to see, she scanned them quickly and squeamishly with her eyes half-shut. Instead of being repulsed, however, the shock she experienced originated from the preview of brilliance she saw.

Several of them were taken on the beach right outside Tommy and Nina's house at the moment the sun began to set. Livia was in a cotton slip just as Nina had said, but it was a see-through gauzy cotton that revealed her figure. There was also a definite sensuousness to her pose—the way Livia looked askance at the camera over her shoulder, her hand resting on her thigh. Even her hair was different. Gone was the customary ribbon on the tail of her braid; her hair hung like a curtain hiding half her face so that she seemed to be flirting with the camera.

In another photo Livia had her back to the camera. She wore a scanty sarong; her arms were extended so that her figure formed the shape of a cross. Her wet hair formed a long wave over her bare shoulder. The black-and-white treatment cast a dark, angry-looking ocean in the background.

Livia came across as being timid and coy at the same time, a metaphorical encapsulation of the complex network of emotions that arises during the transition from girlhood to womanhood.

Caro was speechless.

"What?" Nina begged finally. "I can't stand your silence a second longer."

Caro shook her head slowly. "I don't know what to say except—except that these are extraordinary. I just never suspected you of such talent."

"This is why I'm so mad at Tommy. *I* see these as art. *He* seems not to see anything past the fact that I'm using Livia as my model. I wouldn't do anything to humiliate or hurt her."

Caro nodded in sympathy.

"The normal person," Nina said, "the normal, socially adjusted person—"

"So I suppose I'm not socially adjusted." Tommy spoke through the screen door.

Nina took the cookie sheet out of the oven and slid it onto the countertop with unnecessary clatter. She faced her husband with her hands on her hips. "Where's Livia?"

"Collecting shells." Tommy walked in and immediately approached Caro. "And I suppose being a fellow *artist*"—he hung quotation marks in the air—"you condone these."

"I understand why they might be controversial."

Nina and Tommy reacted simultaneously to Caro's comment.

"At least you're willing to admit there's reason for argument," Tommy said. "More than my wife will concede."

Nina stormed at Caro. "How can you! You said they were genius!"

Caro signaled for a time-out. "Relax, both of you. Nina, do I think they're exquisite? Yes."

Nina snorted in her husband's direction.

"And Tommy, do I think an argument can be made that they're seductive? Yes. I heard you guys arguing the other night."

Nina poked a finger at Tommy. "I told you the whole neighborhood heard."

"Big shit."

"The point is, if I did, then Livia must have," Caro said.

"Then you also know the photos aren't the whole issue," Tommy said.

Nina bolted over to her husband and stood so close that the hiss in her voice reverberated between them. "My career is my business."

"And I'll tell you for the thousandth time it's not fair to use her," Tommy argued.

"Know what bothers me the most, Tommy, is that you used to see the artistic value of my photographs, but now all you do is criticize." Tears collected and dripped onto the curve of her cheekbones.

Nina's weeping did not dilute Tommy's anger. "Would you still be hell-bent on publishing her pictures if she were your daughter?"

Nina stared with assurance at Caro. "Tell him. You know better than he does what I would do."

Caro cleared her throat. "Tommy, I want to remain both your friends. At the same time I have to say that I think Nina would…and should photograph and publish what speaks to her as an artist."

"At any cost?" Tommy asked.

"The only *cost*, as you put it, is the fact that Livia isn't into the modeling. To be honest, I was against forcing her. And then I look at these and see how precisely they capture not only her physical beauty, but that inner essence that makes her a poet, and I—"

"You see?" Nina said to her husband.

"No, I don't. No matter what you or Caro says," Tommy said, and walked out.

"Thank you for sticking up for me," Nina said.

"I have to ask," Caro said. "What *is* your relationship with Livia?"

"She's my only niece. We're a small family, only Carmen and me so we've always been close."

"Then you must have talked to her about—"

"I know how much she hates modeling for me. And though I don't show it, I do feel bad I'm pushing her. And yes, I see this as an opportunity for me. Over the last year, she's matured in such a way… she was always pretty, of course. But not like she is now. So when I read that *Art World Magazine* was sponsoring a portrait exhibition at the National Center for Photography I came up with the idea of a series based around her."

"The National Center puts on major showings. I've been to a few," Caro said.

"That's the point. I wouldn't be doing this for any small-time show."

Caro indicated to Nina that Livia was heading toward the house.

"Will you say something to Livia on my behalf?" Nina asked. "Maybe coming from you, she'll listen."

"Sure, when she comes around to visit next time," Caro said.

The lessons of impermanence, the occasional despair and the muse, so tenuously moored, all visit their needs upon me and I dig deeply for the spiritual utilities that restore me...

~Sally Mann

CHAPTER EIGHT

The next day, Caro's eyebrows rose and a soft expletive escaped her lips as she climbed over the dune to find Livia looking straight at her not more than five feet away from the end of the catwalk. She was lying on a beach towel on her stomach. Her elbows made knobby imprints in the sand and her face rested on her knuckles. Her feet stuck up straight and were crossed at the ankles.

Small-boned and slim, she wore a Speedo, which flattered her body. Caro noticed Livia's toenails had been polished and supposed it had been at Nina's insistence.

"How about helping me with the cabana?" Caro asked.

Livia scrambled to her feet. "I got it." She popped it open against the bank of a particularly mounded dune that was overhung with tall, reedy grasses, and locked the legs in place. Then she ran ahead of Caro, scooped up the cooler, and set it under the cover of the canvas.

It was the perfect time of morning. The sun was at an eastern slant and the only prints on the beach were those left by sandpipers and gulls. Livia picked a piece of grass and chewed its end; the rest of the stem fell away from her mouth in a graceful arc.

"This is a nice surprise," Caro said.

"Aunt Nina's on a shoot."

"Of what?"

"*Home in the Hamptons* asked her to do a piece on the history of how the mill came about in Watermill. I was looking up stuff on the Internet for her and we read it's been there since 1644. Just imagine being one of the original settlers."

"I'm not so sure I want to. I'm more of an 1800's woman myself."

"Maybe then, too," Livia conceded as she drew designs in the sand with her fingers.

The silence between them was calming, a mood Caro was wise enough to fully appreciate. These moments were rare in life, and she made this one special by handing Livia a book, soft-covered and slim. On the front was a woman sitting in a languid pose facing away from the camera, revealing just a hint of a profile. Her hair pinned at the nape of her neck and the collar and bodice of her gown were Victorian in style.

Livia studied the cover front and back, and read the title aloud, "*A Room of One's Own.*"

"Most girls your age wouldn't want anything to do with this. I think you might feel differently. It's not easy though."

Livia flipped through the pages, pausing every now and then to examine some bit of writing. "Thanks."

"I feel like walking. What do you say?" Caro suggested.

Livia got up, the book still in her hand. Before putting it down she said, "Did my aunt tell you it's my birthday tomorrow? Is that why you gave me this?"

Caro's heart filled her chest. Her birthday, how fortuitous! "No, she didn't."

"We're having a celebration supper on Friday. Can you come?"

"Your aunt might be planning something special."

Livia shook her head with such enthusiasm that her braid swung from side to side and coiled itself around her slender neck. "She said she was going to ask you. Besides, I get to choose. It is *my* day."

"*If* your aunt asks, then yes, I'd like to come."

They walked along a good stretch of beach. The tide was receding. A mellow surf coughed up background music rather than the insistent roar of high tide when the waves broke hard at the shoreline. Gulls made mad dives, searching for overturned horseshoe crabs.

Under her straw hat and behind sunglasses, Caro felt oblivious to everything but Livia walking beside her. Once, in an eruption of maternal solicitude, Caro put her arm around Livia's shoulder.

Livia reciprocated by sliding her arm around Caro's waist.

Caro took pride in onlookers seeing them together in such an endearing manner when without notice, she felt herself being pushed into the surf.

Giggling, Livia began splashing Caro.

Caro initiated a counter-attack, when a wave broke over her, and knocked her down.

Livia waded to her. Hand-in-hand, they struggled to get to shore against the battering of consecutive waves. On dry land, they laughed out loud to see a toddler about ten yards away wearing Caro's beached hat, the saturated brim flopping over his ears.

"Where are you going?" Caro asked.

"Get your hat."

"In a minute. Let him play with it for a little while we dry off," Caro said, content to sit right where she was, shoulder to shoulder with Livia, their legs stretched out in front of them.

Later when they were back under cover of the cabana, Livia said, "I took out three of your books from the library. It's all they had."

"Did you read any yet?"

"*Hard Edges of Love.* My aunt told me your husband died." Livia's voice developed in reverence.

"It's okay to talk about him."

"Did you cry when you wrote the poems about him?" Livia asked.

"Not during, but afterward I did when I read one back to myself that I especially liked."

"I bet "Gardening Ways" is one of them. Made Aunt Nina and me both cry."

"I know. He took such pleasure in tending the garden, especially the roses. Our home had vases of flowers year round, either home grown or bought. People used to comment that they were a luxury. They weren't though. They made us smile every time we passed them."

"Aunt Nina's favorites are orchids."

"Orchids are lovely, and seem the perfect flower for your aunt."

"How so?"

"They're sophisticated, if you can imagine such a thing, with their long graceful stems; and each one is quite unique. Like your aunt, she's very talented you know."

Livia looked out to sea. "Did she ask you to talk to me?"

"Yes, she feels bad how much you hate modeling for her." Caro said.

"Then why does she keep insisting that I do it?" Livia asked.

"Because she's an artist and she can't help but appreciate how beautiful you are," Caro said. "It's like your aunt has to split herself in two. Half of her is your aunt who loves and wants to please you. The other half wants to do what's best for her art."

"Yeah, I know. Like with each new husband, my mother says she gets torn between making them happy and making me happy."

"Don't you think their concern shows how much they care about you?"

Livia remained tight-lipped.

"Otherwise they'd both do what they want and not give a hoot. Instead, seems to me that they're trying to find the balance between doing what they need for themselves as well as for you. That's not always easy to achieve."

"Maybe."

"And you love staying with your aunt and uncle, don't you?"

"My friends at school think that living on the ocean is pretty cool."

"I'd have to agree," Caro said.

Just then, Livia stopped and pulled Caro down with her to inspect a sea snail harboring its eggs in the water-packed sand. "Poor things," Livia said. "She laid them when the tide was in and now she's stuck."

Gently mounding sand around the snail, Livia carried it to the water's edge. On the out-going tide, she let it go free, watching as the eggs floated away.

Caro melted inside from her youthful compassion. In that moment, she pretended that Livia was her daughter, an extension of her, created by her in the same way she created a poem from a place she couldn't have explained, maybe couldn't even claim as her own, so little did she understand her own soul. And just as with a poem—which appeared mysteriously, and sometimes beautifully, sometimes darkly, fully formed—the thought of mothering Livia both frightened and exhilarated Caro.

❧

Nina placed a small box in front of Livia, a present from her mom.

"Where is she?" Caro asked Tommy.

"Hong Kong."

Livia tore at the wrapping, searching her aunt and uncle's faces with a curious and touching gleam.

"Go ahead," Nina urged. "We have no idea."

Livia undid the catch of a jewelry box and, holding the gift close to her heart, peeked in. She gasped and her eyes came open like pale moons as she picked out a jade bangle. She slid it on and again, pressed it to her. "This is just like the one that George got Mom. Now I have one, too."

Caro asked, "Who's George?"

"Stepdad," Tommy said.

"It's beautiful," Nina said, as she twisted it around her niece's wrist to get a closer look.

Tommy said, "Mom made a good choice."

"Certainly did," Caro agreed.

"May I call her?" Livia asked.

Tommy calculated the difference in time on his watch. "Yeah, give her a buzz. It's a little after nine in the morning there."

Livia waited for the long-distance connection to go through, all the while staring at her bracelet, and smiling. "Mom, I just opened my gift, and I love it! It is so beautiful. I think Aunt Nina and Caro are very jealous," she teased.

"We are," Nina called out for her sister to hear.

"Happy birthday, darling, and I'm thrilled you're happy with it."

"I am, very much," Livia said.

"You'll have to thank George," Carmen said. "It was his idea. He remembered how much you admired mine."

"I will," Livia said.

"How was your party? So nice that Caro came; you've mentioned her so much in your e-mails."

"Where are you?" Livia asked.

"Hong Kong. In fact—"

"I mean are you in the hotel?"

"Yes," Carmen said. "But I can't stay on long because I'm meeting George for breakfast. He had to leave earlier for a meeting."

"I thought we were going to have a video call for my birthday," Livia said, her voice dropping in disappointment. "Later can we?"

Carmen let out a soft laugh. "Of course not, precious. *Later* will be your middle of the night. Remember I'm twelve hours ahead of you, so my morning is your night and your night is my morning next day. Maybe tomorrow, I'll see how late I get back to the hotel tonight."

"But then my birthday will be past."

"It's okay. I love you," Carmen said.

"Tomorrow," Livia said in a small voice.

"Hopefully, yes. No promises though."

When Livia put down the phone, she went over to her uncle and smothered her face in his chest. Moments later, she said in a teary voice, "Least she doesn't promise anymore."

After Livia excused herself for the night, Nina said, "Wonder, if ever, when Livia's old enough if she'll accept her mother's wandering lifestyle. Because the way it is now, Livia has expectations of Carmen, like the video call, only to be totally let down."

Tommy wiped his palms as if to disengage himself from the subject, and then refilled his wine glass.

Caro thought of Abby so far away in London. "Abby did," she confessed. "You don't ever think it's going to happen, and then one day it does, and your daughter's gone. I feel bad for Carmen without even knowing her, as I do for Livia."

"Don't," Nina said. "Carmen's choosing her life."

"I did, too, because I felt that I had no options. I always believed that I was a writer first and a mother second. Or maybe a wife second, and a mother third. I don't even know. That's one of the reasons I enjoy being with Livia so much. Reminds me of what I missed with Abby."

"And I appreciate the fact that Livia has you in her life this summer. My sister's other marriages didn't upset her as much as this one, or not that I could tell." Nina piled the dishes. "Come help me with coffee," she said to Caro.

When they were in the kitchen, Nina said, "Tommy and I agreed to try and put off any further discussion about Livia until she's gone. So I didn't tell him I submitted the photos to *Art World.*"

"Nina, you didn't," Caro said.

"Shh! I don't care. I'll deal with him if they accept me. In the meantime, please promise you won't say anything?"

"I won't...except that you're crazy."

They rejoined Tommy just as he reached for a second helping of cake. The women exchanged looks of envy that Tommy was immune to gaining weight.

"By the way, what should I wear to Phyllis's party?" Caro asked Nina.

"Dress-down chic," Nina said.

"I don't even know what that means, much less own something that fits the description."

"We'll go shopping one day next week and I'll show you," Nina offered.

"I'll warn you now," Caro said. "I have an intense dislike for shopping, especially for myself, mainly because I circle the racks for untold amounts of time clueless as to what will look right."

"Not to worry. We'll get you and Livia both outfitted. Maybe buy something new for myself," she said and filched a chocolate curl from her husband's plate.

Tommy grimaced in semi-seriousness. "You own dress-down chic already."

"But I'm sure whatever it is, everyone's seen it."

Looking at Caro's hair with a professional eye, Tommy said, "Am I going to see you before the party?"

"I suppose I have to," Caro said with reluctance.

"You do," Nina agreed. "You don't appear to be anywhere near your age, so why announce it with all that gray hair?"

Tommy circled Caro's chair, examining her from different angles. "I'll get my cosmetician to recommend some make-up tips." He held her chin. "If nothing else, liner to bring out your eyes. Matter of fact, I'll slot you in for a day of beauty and you'll have nothing more to do than slip on your party clothes that night."

Nina pushed back her chair. "I'm going to run up and check on Livia."

"I'll help Tommy clean up," Caro offered.

"Thanks," Nina said as she gathered up Livia's presents and mounted the stairs to her room.

"Tell her to stop by tomorrow," Caro offered. "I've got a new poem to show her."

Nina nodded over her shoulder.

Tommy loaded the dishwasher while Caro stored the left-overs. His methodical movements in the kitchen, combined with the residual cooking aromas, reminded her of a favorite uncle who'd entertained her with stories he made up while he dished up Italian dishes. Like Tommy, between him and his wife, her uncle was the softer of the two. "You care for Livia a lot," she said.

"She's sensitive, you know, and Nina, for all her goodness, doesn't understand her. She wants her niece to be tough and outgoing. Unfortunately, those attributes can't be transferred just by willing them on someone."

"If she was stronger, more extroverted, would you be less bothered about the photos?"

"I'm supposed to be sophisticated and cool about different art forms. A canvas painted completely black with a purple circle in the middle of it and titled "Self-Portrait" I've got no argument with. It's ugly but doesn't hurt anyone. A picture of a tattooed porn star, I find less digestible, but she's not related. I treat Livia as I would my own daughter, so yes, I still would have a major problem. I just wish Nina would stick to shooting lighthouses and water mills."

"Wow, you're very clear on how upset you are with Nina, but Tommy—I have to say, that's a pretty selfish attitude. Lighthouses and water mills, come on. You know Nina's better than that."

Tommy stopped what he was doing and turned on Caro. "Did you ever compromise your daughter?"

"In my own ways, yes," Caro said.

"Ever forgive yourself?"

"Not totally," Caro said. "I don't think I ever can."

"My point exactly."

"I don't believe you're worried about Nina regretting—"

"Of course not. I'm concerned about forgiving myself if I don't try and stop her."

There's a period of life when we swallow a knowledge of ourselves and it becomes either good or sour inside.

~PEARL BAILEY

CHAPTER NINE

Caro wrenched the bed sheet and coverlet from the coiled mess around her legs and tucked them up under her chin, her elbows pointing out to either side like airplane wings. Her blanketed and tucked position didn't stop her from bouncing from side to side or from punching the pillow with her fist in frustration minutes later. In the three hours since midnight, she'd drifted off twice as many times, and awakened from a recurring dream.

More like a nightmare, it began with Marcie walking in the park where she had been attacked. Instead of the mugger slamming her with a bat, he covered her eyes with his hands, and exclaimed, "Guess who?" When Marcie peeked, she saw it wasn't her assailant at all. It was Zach!

They didn't spot Caro, who peered from a distance. They didn't kiss. There was no embrace. And yet Caro woke every time sweaty and shaken right at the moment when she found them out.

In reality, Caro had no reason to believe there was anything between Zach and Marcie besides friendship. She reflected on the numerous occasions the three of them had been together. After Marcie's divorce, she melded into their family seamlessly. They didn't have to invite her to anything; it was expected that she'd be there, and most of the time she was.

Often, on weekends, Marcie stayed over, bringing an overnight bag. After a while, so many of her clothes had accumulated at the apartment that one day when Caro was doing the laundry, she'd laughed to herself at the number of Marcie's items she was washing.

Caro sat upright, drew her knees in and hugged them as she recalled the many nights she had holed herself up in her study to write. Intermittent chords of laughter would drift up the circular staircase like curlicues of cigarette smoke and she'd raise the volume on whatever mood music she had on so as not to lose focus.

She'd never been jealous of them. Quite the opposite, she was a dedicated artist and Marcie's friendship with Zach alleviated her guilt for not spending the evenings with him watching reruns of *Seinfeld* and *Sex and the City*.

Zach and Marcie? The only other person she loved more was her daughter. They wouldn't have cheated on Caro. She drew out the oversized T-shirt in front of her—U.S. Open, '96. She'd known Marcie only six months. Nevertheless, when Zach found out she was an obsessive Andre Agassi fan, he'd insisted she tag along to Queens with them to attend the grand-slam tennis event. Marcie had bought him the T-shirt in appreciation.

Caro went into the kitchen, switching on lights. Standing with the refrigerator door open, she was deciding whether to drink iced tea or a beer, when a staggering thought seized her heart and slid up to her throat.

Zach had been at a job site when he'd suffered his heart attack. By the time Caro had received the phone call and then driven to the hospital, he was already undergoing surgery to repair an aortic aneurysm. Afterward, the doctors had assured her the prognosis looked hopeful. It took Zach only twenty-eight hours to prove them wrong.

Marcie had arrived at the hospital shortly after Caro and had remained until the end. In the last hour before Zach died, he'd asked to see Marcie alone. At the time, Caro had imagined that he wanted to extract a promise from Marcie that she'd look after his wife and daughter. She was so upset—who knew what she was thinking, or why. But that was it.

And when Marcie emerged from the room, her eyes red from crying, Caro asked about the piece of paper crushed in Marcie's fist. Marcie had denied its importance; a tissue, she'd said. But a circle of red darkened around her neck like a collar and stained her cheeks and she'd hurried off down the hall.

Although over the next weeks Marcie's obfuscation had niggled at Caro, in her grief the incident had gotten lost. Now she contemplated with a studied fierceness what that paper could have been—what had it contained?

Agitated by her insomnia and her irrational thoughts, Caro dialed Abby's number, hoping that her daughter's voice would calm her.

"Mom, this is the third time this month you're calling in the middle of your night. Are you all right?"

"I had bad dreams about Marcie," Caro said.

"Did you want to talk about it?"

"It's just that I haven't been able to settle down to anything since she died. I haven't written, and now I'm getting nightmares. Seems like Livia's the only person I feel completely sane with."

"And me?" Abby said.

"You know what I mean. Out of the people I see here."

"Maybe that's your problem. Except for her aunt and uncle, you don't mention anyone else *but* her. You need to socialize. What is it that you do with her anyway?"

Caro was defensive. "I mentor her."

"In what?"

"Poetry mostly. She has great potential. More important, I understand her and she appreciates that."

"That's fine, but nobody mentors twenty-four seven," Abby said.

"There's no one else to socialize with. Besides, I'd compare everyone to Marcie."

"That's totally understandable. That's why you need to give yourself a push. You know how easy it is for you to isolate."

"Easy as it is for you to give advice. What I need is a little sympathy."

Abby checked the time; she had to get ready for work, and so she ignored her mother's barb. "I'm sorry, Mom. Losing Marcie's been hard."

Caro felt herself in the grips of a bad mood, and itching to fight with her daughter. "That's all you can say? Maybe if you lost someone close to you—"

"Does losing my dad count?" Abby shot back.

"No, he was family. I mean someone you choose especially to be a best friend, that you can depend on and talk to and…"

"I'm getting off," Abby said.

"Not now you're not. I'm still talking," Caro snapped.

"Fuck, Mom! You want to pick a fight, go find your young school friend," Abby said, and hung up.

Caro was glad not to talk to her daughter any longer. How dare Abby implicate Livia in their disagreement. Livia was fast becoming a part of Caro's daily routine, and *finding* her was exactly what Caro needed.

By first light, Caro was walking along the beach as the sun moved in and out of a rosy, purplish haze. A beautiful day was inevitable for even now she detected the globular field of yellow heat behind the low cloud cover. She walked quickly, mentally stamping out her argument with her daughter the night before with each definitive footprint she made in the hard-packed sand.

She thought of Livia instead. Indeed, she couldn't stop thinking about the girl. She didn't understand how she could be falling in love with the teen. And yet, she couldn't get around the hard truth—she did love her.

Caro didn't realize how far she'd walked until she came upon the Hampton Bay Bridge. On the other side was Lacey's, a coffee shop that opened at four, though most of its customers, at that hour, were fishermen.

It was nothing more than a shack with a screened-in porch for sitting. There was additional seating outside, but the plastic chairs were still wet with dew and turned seat-side-down on the tabletops. The pungent smells of fish, bait, and diesel fuel brought Caro back to the living.

Caro gave her order at the counter and stepped into line with the other patrons who were waiting for their food. Suddenly, she muttered "Shit!" and dug in the pockets of her hoodie for money, knowing she'd forgotten to bring any. "Excuse me. Excuse me," she said repeatedly as she inched her way to where she'd placed her order—and found herself face to face with Nina.

"Oh, thank God, how great to meet you here," Caro said. "I forgot my wallet. Do you have a few dollars to spare?"

"Sure. I'm just getting a second cup of coffee. Livia's over there," she said and pointed to a table along the wall. "I'll grab your order when it comes up."

"Livia's here?"

"Yeah, like I said, over there."

"What are you doing up and out this early?" Caro asked Livia.

"We were at the docks before dawn to photograph a fisherman who hooked a twelve-foot great white shark yesterday. The shark had been kept on ice overnight especially for the shoot. It was amazing."

"I have to agree, it was pretty extraordinary," Nina said as she placed the coffee and food on the table. "What's your story, Caro?"

Caro shook her head. "I just started walking this morning and—"

"*Walking*, did you say?"

"I know," Caro said. "I kind of had it on autopilot."

"Guess so. Anyway, I was going to call you later to ask if you want to come to Queens with me tomorrow. I'm getting a tattoo as a surprise for Tommy for our anniversary next week. I really want things to ease up between us." She whispered the last comment behind her hand at the same moment Livia left the table to fetch syrup from the counter.

"Can I tell?" Livia asked as she prepared her pancakes.

"Go ahead," her aunt said.

"The tattoo is of an angel with very long hair. She's on tiptoes with clouds below her, and reaching up to a star. The hair is for Uncle Tommy being a stylist, and his name is written in the clouds."

"Where are you putting it? And how big?" Caro asked.

"A three-by-three circle on my shoulder."

"Hope he loves it." Caro's attention was on Livia. The newly risen sun shone through the window screens, dispersing particles of light like glitter across her face.

"Do you have any tattoos, Caro?" Nina asked.

"Actually, I *almost* got one once. And have thought about it now and then."

"When? What happened that you didn't?" Livia sat forward, her expression full of anticipation.

"Never had the courage, I guess. And my husband didn't like them on women."

"Get one now with me," Nina said.

"Don't think so. Not on this old body of mine," Caro said.

Livia's enthusiasm and curiosity about the subject produced a pale blush on her cheeks. "What would you get if you did?"

Caro didn't hesitate. "A long-stemmed lotus in full bloom with the word *infinity* written in black Chinese characters above it. I'd have it done right here." She indicated her right hip. "And another small one on my inner wrist."

"Seems like you've thought about it more than only every once in a while."

Caro remained neutral. "Like I said, not on this body."

Nina urged, "Come be my support anyway?"

"Sure, what time?"

"My appointment's at two. But I figure we'll leave about noon so we have time to get lunch before. I know a great Italian deli nearby."

"Coming too?" Caro asked Livia.

"Wouldn't miss it. Maybe I'll get a tattoo."

"Don't get any ideas," her aunt cautioned. "Your mom's not into tattoos."

"Mom's not here," Livia said in a tone of finality.

Caro asked Livia, "What are you doing for the rest of the day?"

Livia looked to her aunt for an answer.

"Nothing planned yet, but we need to decide when we're going clothes shopping for Phyllis's party."

Caro begged off. "Another day."

"You sound like someone else I know," Nina complained.

Caro winked at Livia, whose face lit into a smile.

"Well," Caro said, "Sweetwater Books is sponsoring an open-mike poetry reading tonight. Thought you might want to go?"

"Are you reading?" Livia asked.

"Maybe, I haven't decided yet."

"I'd like to. What about you, Aunt Nina?"

"Thanks, but I'll leave the poetry to you two."

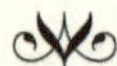

The reading was at the gazebo on the village green. As Caro and Livia walked from the car with thermoses and blankets, Caro felt the pride of having Livia with her. People paused in their conversations to stare at the girl, whose skin, in the light of the late-day sun, appeared almost iridescent.

"It's crowded already," Livia said. "Want me to run ahead to get a good spot?"

"You don't have to and really, I don't feel like climbing over a lot of people. We'll find a place out of the main throng," Caro said and steered Livia off to one side, near the forsythia that hedged the property.

Caro positioned herself slightly behind Livia so she could look upon her and keep her eyes on the stage at the same time. Not long ago, Abby had cautioned her that she needed a life, but she wanted little else than Livia's company; it seemed that simple. And her ambition to mentor Livia seemed to fade in the face of her growing feelings.

Within a short time, Ian Finch, the owner of Sweetwater Books, began the proceedings with a brief welcome, then introduced the first reader, a local poet whose book Ian had displayed in the window of his store.

Caro was the third to read. Ian introduced her as "a cherished poet, and winner of numerous prestigious awards, including the Pulitzer Prize in 1995 for her collection, *Primal Landscapes.*" He continued, "Ms. Barrone is at work on a new collection, *In Search of Eros,* from which she will read tonight's selection entitled, "Desire." Ms. Barrone." Ian led the audience in applause.

Caro's style of poetic recitation was purposeful, almost pensive, as if she was new to the work and intent on capturing each nuance of language, dallying over the words; strung together they became the verses that hung like stars over the bandstand.

When she recited the closing lines of the poem, she closed her eyes. *"...deeply submerged, I am in a world of halcyon darkness where a warm greenness caresses my body in undisclosed compassion."*

Livia was on her feet clapping when Caro rejoined her.

Although the night was mild, when darkness settled a stiff breeze came off the ocean. Anticipating the cool-down, Caro had made hot chocolate for Livia and Irish coffee for herself. She filled thermos cups and spread out a fabric napkin with oatmeal cookies.

At the close of another reader's poem, Livia asked, "What does languorous mean? I love the sound of it."

"Listless, lethargic...or having a dreamy quality to something," Caro said.

"Languorous," Livia repeated the newly learned word. "What a languorous evening this is."

Caro smiled. "Or, what a wonderfully languorous expression Livia has on her face."

As the readings progressed, they cheered at the good ones and screwed up their faces in distaste at the bad poems, but applauded nonetheless. During intermission they wandered among the crowd. A few people addressed Caro with the knowing "hello" of recognition.

When they returned to their blanket, Caro zipped up her jacket and leaned on her elbows. She let her head fall back on her shoulders. Above the lampposts that bracketed the gardens and the white Christmas lights that outlined the gazebo, the sky was heavy with stars. "What a lovely night," she said.

As Ian took the stage and announced the program for the second half of the evening, Livia leaned over and whispered to Caro, "In the poem you read tonight everything takes place in the dark, underwater. Is that why you feel compassion? Because the desire has to be in secret, *undisclosed?*" Livia cupped her hand over Caro's ear when she continued. "Seems like the desire has something to do with sex; I just don't know what."

Livia's mouth was so close to Caro's ear that Caro felt her breath and delighted in the chocolaty scent. It was the fragrance of youth. "Desire sometimes implies sexual desire. But it also means a great longing for something, like a person craving to go home after an extended journey away."

Livia leaned in toward Caro, prepared to build on her question when Caro put her finger to her lips and, nodding toward the performer on stage, whispered, "Later."

In truth, she was hoping Livia would forget about pursuing further discussion. Caro's own sexual feelings were so confused. Lately, the most innocent bodily gesture of Livia's stirred Caro in ways that made her want to reciprocate—and also made her crush the impulse. Even now the sight of Livia stretched out on the blanket, her eyelids quivering with sleepiness, caused Caro to tremble. She sat on her hands so she wouldn't be tempted to stroke the girl's face.

Later, when Caro brought Livia home, Nina answered the door.

"Hi," Livia said, and gave her aunt a peck on the cheek in greeting. Turning back to Caro, she startled her with a heartfelt hug before disappearing inside.

Caro declined Nina's offer for a nightcap. Feeling deliciously alone, she walked down to the beach. The tide was going out, and she walked out a long ways, her feet sloshing in the saturated sand. With every few steps, she relived the sensation of Livia's arms around her, the brief euphoria that erupted from her heart in little waves and came out in goose bumps on her flesh.

It is not sex that gives the pleasure, but the lover.

~Marge Piercy

CHAPTER TEN

Sheets of pre-made tattoo templates, called flash, covered the walls in systematic categorization of the main styles of tattooing: old school, tribal, ethnic, Celtic, Asian, and fantasy. The specific type often determined whether the work displayed best in black and white or color. Autographed pictures of celebrities who'd gotten their tattoos done at Sean Z's Tattoos demonstrated the most popular selections.

Now, as Caro, Livia, and Nina waited for him to call her in, they ogled their favorite stars. Livia wandered across to the Asian section and began scanning the flash with names written in Chinese calligraphy. She found the equivalent of "Livia" in "Olivia" and to her surprise "Nina" was there as well. She was scrolling through the alphabet when Caro joined her. "Yours wasn't here," she said.

"That might be because Caro is short for Caroline."

"Oh, I passed Caroline before, and look here—Zach."

Caro followed to where Livia indicated on the wall. "That's not his."

"Yes," Livia insisted. "I saw the exact design over there, too."

Caro walked to where Livia pointed, her face leaching of color with each step. The tattoo on the board with Zach's name, was Marcie's tattoo.

Caro felt a stabbing deep inside of her at the sudden souring of a marriage and a friendship. When Zach died, Marcie's tears hadn't been a sympathetic consequence of Caro's grief. Rather, she was lamenting with Caro—a lover, a second wife. Her visionary dreams she'd had weeks earlier of Zach and Marcie together were true after all.

Livia's face registered alarm. "What's wrong?"

Caro ran out of the shop and didn't stop running until she collapsed on a bench three blocks away, nearly knocking into an elderly woman. She tried to stabilize her quaking body and swallow her sobs. How blind not to have known what was going on? Then again, why not? They had been her husband and her closest confidante. She'd trusted them. Images of them together made her stomach lurch until she felt she was going to vomit.

As much as she wanted to, she also knew she couldn't stay where she was but must return to the tattoo shop; Nina and Livia would be worried. She got up slowly, cautiously, and began walking back to the shop.

Nina and Livia were outside on the sidewalk, searching up and down the street. When Caro drew within their sight, they ran to her, each grabbing an elbow, and escorted her back to the car.

Caro cried, "What about your tattoo? Your surprise for Tommy?"

"Not to worry," Nina said. "Have some water and try to settle down."

The trio was silent except for Caro's weeping. When she'd calmed down, Nina asked, "Want to talk about it?"

"Marcie had a tattoo on her ankle of Chinese letters. When I asked her their meaning she said they spelled out her name.

But…but it was really Zach's name. Know how long she got it before he died?"

Nina took Caro's hand, and shook her head.

"Four years. It's a long time, right? Four years. And how long before that did they really start their affair?" Caro swallowed a fresh attack of tears. "I mean, you just don't get a tattoo right away. A year…two years…"

Livia put her hand on Caro's shoulder. "I'm sorry."

"I can't know what you're feeling," Nina said, "but I do know it won't do any good to torment yourself like this. Do a few months more or less really matter?"

"I need to go home," Caro said quietly.

Caro telephoned Abby, not stopping to consider the time difference.

"I know how much you loved your father," Caro blurted out. "Adored him, but you're the only person I can talk to."

"Mom, what are you talking about? It's after midnight."

"I don't know how to start. Your father and Marcie…"

Silence.

"Abby, help me. Are you there?"

"I'm trying to think of an answer," Abby said. "I'm sorry."

And then Caro knew. "How is that possible? I'm having a hard time understanding. Believing. You knew and didn't tell me!" Her sentences came out in uneven fragments.

"I didn't know what to say, Mom. Try to understand my position. You're right, I adored Dad and then to find out that he was a…cheater. The whole thing made me sick."

"All the more reason you needed to tell me, for both of us," Caro said.

"I thought I was saving you from a lot of heartache. You loved Marcie, and I didn't want to take that away from you. And then Dad died, and I saw no justification in telling you."

"Bullshit! Bullshit! Bullshit! You didn't tell me because you didn't want to deal with me."

"That's not true," Abby said.

"Do me a favor, Abby. I just found out that my husband and my best friend were fucking each other behind my back. So cut me some slack."

"How did you find out? Why now?" Abby asked.

Caro laughed, a sour sound. "Marcie's tattoo. It was your father's name, and parading around in front of me the whole time. Did you know about the tattoo?"

"No."

"Well…at least that's something you didn't have to keep secret—"

"Wahoo, how great for me. The truth is, you didn't want to know about any one of us."

"How can you insinuate I didn't want to be a part of your life?"

"Easy. You shut your eyes and covered your ears. They were never discreet, cozying up to each other in front of the TV, and calling each other, hon….Christ! Didn't it ever bother you that Marcie wore lace to bed at night instead of cotton?"

Abby's observations stilled Caro. True, they were an assault to whatever self-esteem Caro had left about having been an emotionally present participant in her family. More odious was Abby's meanness in telling her.

Caro said, "Whatever I chose to see or not see doesn't give you the right to judge or chastise me. I'm your mother. No matter what, I deserve your respect."

"No, you don't. Respect, like love, is earned. And I have every right to be angry because you didn't do any better by me than you did them. You were as absent a mother and wife emotionally as they come. Your words, Mom—they were fucking each other behind your back."

"That's enough, Abby! It's easy to beat me up time and time again instead of owning up to your own actions. Because let me tell you, it's getting old."

"I never wronged you," Abby challenged.

"Ran away for one. Living in the same town was too close. You had to move across the ocean. Would you be living in London if your father was still alive?"

"Time to get off, Mother. Maybe you'll get an idea for a poem out of this."

"You're running again," Caro said.

Abby hung up.

In spite of her anger, Caro understood her daughter's propensity for running away from her and Zach. She'd learned from the best. Caro was an expert at blindly moving forward through family preoccupations and obstacles, and she would have relied on those same psychological tools again to ease through this conflict with Abby.

The discovery of Zach's affair with Marcie, still surreal even several days later, showed her that keeping her distance with Abby didn't accomplish anything in their relationship and hurt just as much.

She'd already left a voice-mail for her daughter suggesting another call. In addition, she purchased her airline tickets for Abby's birthday, compromising with herself by staying away only five days instead of the original plan of two weeks, so as not to be separated from Livia for too long.

Caro looked upon her affection for Livia, and the girl's reciprocity, as a blessed gift amid the grief of loss and betrayal over the last months. She seemed to touch something in Caro that was like soothing salve over a bruise. That morning, Caro came across a letter the poet Rilke wrote to his student, which she intended to share with Livia.

In it, Rilke counseled the young man about the great gift of sadness being a collection of solitary moments when everything within withdraws, and out of which arises something new, a new sense of direction, a new self. And no matter how much you want to believe nothing has changed, he wrote, disbelief is an impossibility. A great deal inside has been transformed.

The message of transformation motivated Caro to telephone Nina to go shopping for Phyllis's party. And then there was her appointment with Tommy. On Saturday night she would appear a newly fashioned woman.

Some day you will be old enough to start reading fairy tales again.

~C.S. Lewis

CHAPTER ELEVEN

Tommy held up a color chart to Caro's head and sorted through the hair swatches for an attractive match. "I don't think we should go as light as your natural color. What do you think of adding an auburn tint? Add luminance to your pale eyes and complexion while giving you some definition around the face."

"You're not talking red. I've had that before and hated it," Caro said.

"Heavens no. Red would be dreadful. Like I said, the auburn will act only as a highlight. As for the style ..." He combed through her hair with his fingers from the nape up, "...there's not much to work with. I'd say since it's so chopped already, the best thing is to take it super short in a style that makes a statement."

Caro offered him a weak nod. Her commitment to being a "new woman" was draining quickly now that she was actually involved in the process. She'd forgotten what it was like to have stylists and aestheticians pucker their brows when confronted with her thin hair and washed-out complexion. She groaned inwardly and stiffened.

Tommy squeezed her shoulders. "You're going to be fine. Now off with Lily here for your facial."

Caro rose obediently and allowed herself to be taken through the earth-colored doors overhung with hand-painted vines and the legend *Serenity* in italicized script. Once inside, she was pleasantly surprised. The heady scent of herbs accompanied by the liquid strains of nature music made her feel weightless. She breathed without tension, long slow intakes of the perfumed air.

At the completion of her treatments, she regretted having to re-enter the ammonia-scented world of the salon with its walls of steel and glass and the ring of mirrors in which Caro saw herself in duplicate and triplicate.

Tommy applied the dye to her hair and eyebrows and sat her under a heating element that looked vaguely like the planet Saturn. In the harsh light that emanated from the encircling bulb Caro was struck by how the dye created a freakish halo around her face resembling car engine oil. Her eyebrows leaked at the edges. The mawkish color accentuated the worry lines between her eyes that had gutted deep in the last few years, a family legacy on her mother's side. Every woman in the family had them, along with an uneven and vague lip line.

Would having gray hair even matter if love was of the spirit and not of form? At the very least, coloring the hair eased the pain of having arrived at a certain age. Caro shifted uncomfortably; either way she pitied herself because the result, however successful, would be fleeting and illusory—just like her experiences of love with Zach and Marcie.

As Tommy had promised, Caro returned home a finished product and didn't have to do anything except redo her lipstick and get dressed. When she'd gone shopping with Nina they had rummaged through half a dozen boutique shops until Nina had come across just the right outfit.

Staring at her reflection in the full-length mirror, Caro felt at home with herself in the simplicity and sparkle of a simple black dress with pearls.

Nina and Tommy had offered to escort her to the party so she wouldn't have to make a solo entrance. Livia had called minutes before to say they were leaving as soon as her aunt made a final check of her makeup. What was Livia going to think of Caro's refashioned look?

Caro's self-consciousness about her appearance didn't supersede her vision of how Livia was going to look. Nina had selected a sea-green dress with spaghetti straps and a cummerbund-style belt trimmed in pink, which took the eye away from Livia's small bosom and accentuated her tiny waist and straight back. The short length showed off her legs. The outfit was a blend of youthful sophistication.

When the trio arrived, Livia's enthusiastic expression reflected her compliment, "You look beautiful. Uncle Tommy said you did."

Caro squeezed Livia. "I'm glad you like it."

"The short hair is genius," Nina said to Tommy, and then to Caro, "You look fabulous."

"Thanks, but let me see *you,*" Caro said and turned Livia around. Nina had French-braided her hair. The wispy bangs and free-floating tendrils bounced at the corners of her eyes, star-lit ovals that this evening appeared to have an ocean of green in them. "I think your aunt and uncle did excellent by us."

Well into her eighties, Phyllis's sharp blue eyes and quiet elegance were still her hallmark qualities that prompted strangers to take notice, and new acquaintances, to delight in getting to know her.

Upon meeting Caro, Phyllis had taken her hand and in a warm embrace and said, "What a delight, Caro. Thanks so much for coming."

Caro became an instant fan. She had never been the guest of honor at such a lavish gathering—sixty of Phyllis's *closest* friends—when she didn't have to get up at some point in the evening and earn her supper by giving a reading. On this occasion, she was able to relax into the party atmosphere and enjoy mingling with the other guests.

She'd chatted with several people, but was standing alone when Tommy and Nina came up to her in tow with Livia; a woman and young girl also joined them.

"Caro, this is Deena Michaels and her daughter, Beatrice," Tommy said. "Deena and I know each other from high school. Deserted us when she got married."

"Nice to meet you," Caro said to Deena. And then to Beatrice, "Hello."

Deena shook Caro's hand. "And now I'm divorced, so here I am back again. Except that this time, I've got company," she said, embracing her daughter.

"This is the first opportunity we've had a chance to introduce Livia and Beatrice to each other," Nina said to Caro.

The girls smiled at each other, and looking at them side by side, Caro was struck by their appearance. They were a case in contrast: for as pretty and appealing Livia was, Beatrice was plain. Her smile was her single asset; it seemed to emanate a warmth that came from her heart.

"What do you like to do, Beatrice?" Caro asked.

"Anything to do with the water. Surf, mostly."

"Beatrice is saving up for a surf board," Livia said.

"Very impressive," Caro said. "I don't imagine they're very cheap."

"They're not. That's why my dad is making me buy it with my own money," Beatrice said. "He has a pool business so he pays me for helping him out."

"That must keep you busy," Tommy said.

"Not too bad," Beatrice said. "I go out with him three mornings a week. The rest of the time, I'm free."

"Well, Beatrice, anytime you want to visit, please do," Nina said. "You and Livia might turn out to be great company for each other."

"Thanks," Beatrice said. She turned to Livia. "Want to go out and walk around?"

"Sure," Livia said.

"Come on," Beatrice said, grabbing Livia's hand and guiding her through the mill of guests.

Caro stared after the girls, already chatting animatedly. And all of a sudden, she felt sick to her stomach. A friendship between the two of them would severely impinge on her time with Livia. This thought made Caro hate Beatrice. Why didn't she and her mother stay in Rhode Island?

The truth was, Caro was jealous of their fun, and of the freedom Beatrice had to lightheartedly manhandle her friend. Caro was demonstrative by nature and in normal conversation thought nothing of pressing a wrist or caressing an arm even with people she'd just met.

Moral to the point of being borderline prudish, she was scrupulous, however, about avoiding close physical contact with Livia. Since her husband's death, she'd never been interested in remarrying or finding a male companion. Discovering his affair, however, had instigated a desire to let go and be bad. She'd learned that keeping her prim behavior intact all her life had only led her to misery.

The fact, however, that Livia was the cause of her sexual stirrings horrified Caro. And yet, she could not deny them. Even now, as she stole looks at Livia she saw a girl on the cusp of young adulthood—still the tomboy, but in a flirty, feminine package—and her moral and ethical reserves weakened. A momentary image of kissing Livia rose to her consciousness. She immediately crushed it.

To raise, to elevate, to endorse with timeless reverence the image of woman, has been my mission—the reason for my work.

~Ruth Bernhard

CHAPTER TWELVE

Sexless. Innocent. Truthful.

Perfect love in its simplest form begins with an attraction to a beautiful object, but then is raised beyond the body, to its highest form—spirit.

This was the dictum Caro recited and meditated on as she continued to smother thoughts and impulses regarding Livia that were even mildly suggestive. The current arrangement between them was proving advantageous for both of them: mad at Abby, and sorry for the love she'd wasted on Zach and Marcie, Caro was happy to bestow her love on Livia.

As for Livia, she reveled in the unconditional affection of a maternal figure, especially one who understood without question the eccentricity of her poetic sensibilities.

Consequently, in the days that followed Phyllis's party, Caro came to depend on Livia's presence for her sanity. Her nights were a fragmentary progression of hours between fitful sleep and blurry wakefulness. Marcie and Zach appeared in disquieting reveries.

The rhythm of Caro's days often got underway before daybreak. Huddled under a comforter, she contentedly watched the lazy strokes of pink and purple filter across the sky. In slowly widening increments, the sea separated itself out, a bullish companion as it heaved itself endlessly forward to the shore. Caro appreciated the forthright action of the swift-moving tides because their movement represented the daily swelling of enthusiasm as the minutes edged toward nine or ten when Livia would appear.

During this early hour Caro recalled from the day before Livia's sweet smile that Caro could now coax out of her quite easily. It was a smile that produced the hint of dimples on her cheeks. Or she'd hear again Livia reading a poem from a volume they'd chosen on one of their trips to the library. Better yet, the young poet would read one of her own, and Caro would hang on to every word. She'd dissect it not for its literary worth as much as to discern Livia's moods.

The previous afternoon, Livia had brought a poem she'd written about ants. The title was "Lamentation," another ode to her absent mother. Livia had read:

sand ants
with
long legs
bent at ninety degree
sharp angles
scurry up and
down endless mounds of sand seemingly going
no where
like my mother
doing the same thing
only at a much slower pace

Afterward, she confessed in a shaky voice that she'd felt sad to think that no matter how fast ants scuttle up and down on the beach, the time it takes them to cover two or three yards is accomplished by adults in a second with one long stride.

Livia continued, "Now multiply the distances humans travel and in the same time the ants haven't gotten anywhere at all because they keep going around the same miniature sand dunes."

"But how do you relate that to your life?" Caro had inquired.

"I think of all the miles Mom travels but they don't get her any closer to me because she keeps going in the same circles, just like the ants."

"Not having your mother around is a very real thing to lament," Caro had offered, at the same time wishing Carmen would never return.

Hours with Livia were what Caro lived for and gave all of her concentration to, all the while attentive to the fact that she had no existence other than what she took from her relationship with Livia.

She didn't plan anything unless the activity was of a kind that could include Livia. She didn't socialize with anyone except for Nina and Tommy, because on those occasions, Livia was there as well.

On the beach, Caro was usually in sight of Livia's brown legs skipping through the breakers or her head bobbing in the waves; she gazed upon Livia sunbathing, the girl's skin iridescent with tanning oil.

As a voyeur—a poet—Caro was skilled at enjoying long, sidelong glances from her elevated position on the dune or from inside her portable cabana. Caro knew every line and plane of her protégé's body, whether in motion, or in stillness, and from her vantage points the magnificence of the sun and sea and sky were but mere background for Livia's graceful progress in the world.

Caro didn't see a problem with her life until now, when she realized that the structure of her days was a claustrophobic repeat of when Zach and Marcie were alive. Except that instead of concentrating her attention and energy on her poetry, she focused on Livia.

Abby had been right to say that Caro didn't see what was going on between her husband and best friend. How could she when she lived most of her time in the limited world of her study?

There were some small intimacies that she hadn't missed, just not readily acknowledged until reviewing them in retrospect. Once, on a rare evening when Caro had joined them to watch a talk show, the TV host had joked to his guest.

"Let me get this straight," the host had said. "Rather than put your socks on both feet, followed by your shoes, you do one foot completely and then do the other."

"Even to tying up the laces," the guest had said.

Caro had opened her mouth to comment.

Marcie had been quicker. "That's so weird, Zach. Could be you he's talking about."

"Don't I wish I was a rich celebrity," Zach had quipped.

Not until the next day did the question register in Caro's mind: how would Marcie know in what order her husband put on his socks and shoes?

When Caro confronted Marcie, she'd said, "Every time he goes to the gym."

Marcie's explanation was satisfactory enough. Caro made Zach keep his sneakers in the laundry room so he was in full view of anyone who happened to be in the kitchen when he put them on. Still, Caro experienced an uneasiness in the brief bluntness of Marcie's reply.

"I have a favor to ask," Nina was saying to Caro. They were sitting on Caro's deck. "Tommy and I were wondering if you'd mind having Livia sleep over Saturday night. Some friends invited us to stay on their boat, and there's a slight chance we might not get back until Monday."

"Of course," Caro said.

"Thanks. Also," Nina said, her expression leveling, "I need to talk to you."

"Okay."

"The editor from *Art World* contacted me."

Caro sat up straighter. "And?"

"At first I was disappointed because he began by declining to publish the photos—"

"Oh, no," Caro began…

"—because his magazine is covering an upcoming exhibition at the National Center for Photography called "Changing Faces of Youth." Although most of the artists have been slotted, he wants to push to have my photos of Livia included."

"Wow! How amazing for you!"

"It is a huge deal. And then, there's Tommy," Nina said glumly. "I know I come off like a bitch sometimes, but I do love him. We try to make believe that we're not angry at each other for me wanting to publish the photos of Livia, but we both know we are. So we're politely distant. And now, this."

"But, Nina, it's not like you weren't aware of how Tommy felt before you submitted the photos. In all honesty, you had to figure you had a shot at *Art World* liking your work otherwise you wouldn't have sent them."

Nina pouted. "You're always against me."

"There's an expression that my father used to use—either shit or get off the pot."

Nina jumped up in a huff.

"Oh, sit down," Caro said. "It's decision time, Nina. The way I see your situation is to either commit one hundred percent to your art, which means moving forward with *Art World, or* forget about the exhibition and go back to your life pre-Livia photos, and make Tommy happy."

"Thanks much for the options," Nina said.

"I'll accept your slight hostility because I understand how you struggle with this," Caro said.

Nina looked at Caro in earnest. "If you had to do your marriage over again, would you do it the same? I mean, do you think that's why your husband cheated on you—because he was unhappy, second-fiddle to your career?"

"I would be more like you," Caro said.

Nina raised her eyebrows. "Me?"

Caro nodded. "You're aware of the pitfalls; you ponder long and hard how your choices might affect your marriage. I never did that. I steamrolled my way through a teaching and a writing career without much forethought. That's why I believe once you make up your mind, whatever happens you'll be fine."

"And if Tommy goes the route that Zach did and finds someone else..."

"Like I said, if you can walk away from the exhibition, and be okay with that decision, so be it."

May we agree that private life is irrelevant?
Multiple, mixed, ambiguous at best—
out of it we try to fashion the crystal
clear, the singular...

~MAY SARTON

CHAPTER THIRTEEN

Caro put freshly cut flowers in the guest room. She'd already talked to Nina about snack foods that Livia preferred and had rented two of Livia's favorite movies, *Fried Green Tomatoes* and *Benny & Joon*. Caro was thinking about the sleepover when Nina appeared on the deck, rapping on the glass.

"There's been a change in plans," Nina said.

Caro slid open the doors and stepped outside. "What?"

"The friends with the boat invited Beatrice's mother and boyfriend along. So, either you get both girls or, if you don't want to—which is totally fine—Beatrice's older sister will take them."

Caro didn't mean to show how miffed she was, but her disappointment was so instantaneous at having to share Livia that she crossed her arms over her chest and threw out her bottom lip.

"Okay, okay, the girls will go to Beatrice's sister," Nina said. "I only asked."

"It's not that," Caro said.

"Then what?"

"I really was looking forward to spending the evening with Livia alone."

"Whatever for? I thought you'd be relived that she'd have company," Nina said.

"Livia's company for *me*. Besides the poetry…I like having her around. She's sweet. Why do I have to explain?"

"You don't. You're the one making a thing about this," Nina said in frustration. "Okay, let's start all over again. Do you want them here or not?"

"Yes," Caro said.

After Caro and the girls had changed into their pajamas, they went outside onto the deck. Caro lazed on the lounge, half-dozing with a glass of Riesling, and the girls were tucked together on the swinging bench, twin soda cans next to them on the floor.

They gazed up at the sky, blue-black with a white full moon so vivid they could make out the fine etching of its craters. Beatrice had spotted a shooting star earlier—the reason for their vigil—and now they waited for another. Every so often they told a corny joke in between chatter about who they'd spotted on the beach that day.

Notwithstanding Caro's jealousy at having to share Livia, she had to admit that the two of them were a good match in spite of their differences. In a bittersweet way they reminded Caro of how it had been with Marcie.

She was thankful that she hadn't learned about the affair with Zach until after Marcie had died. She had no barometer with which to gauge how she would've handled the situation. If she had to give her daughter advice for a similar situation, she would encourage her to cut her losses and move on. There would be no more accurate way of saying it, and no safer way to keep her heart from getting broken a second time.

Her only regret that evening was that she was not swinging next to Livia, maybe even with her arm in casual repose along the back of the bench, barely skimming Livia's soft shoulders.

The chains from which the swing hung came to a grating halt and the girls sprang from their seats in unison.

"We're going to take a walk," Livia said.

Caro also stood up and did a quick survey up and down the beach. The firelight from a few marshmallow roasts still burned; other than those, and the infrequent burst of laughter from one or another resident enjoying late night drinks on their decks, the beach was empty.

"We'll be fine," offered Beatrice.

"I'll go in and set up the movie. Which one do you want first?"

After a brief conference with Beatrice, Livia sang out, "Johnny Depp," as she kicked off her flip-flops and headed over the dune with Beatrice in close pursuit.

It had been almost a month since Caro had dedicated herself body and soul to Livia—and about two weeks since Beatrice began joining them on a regular basis. That afternoon Caro had driven the girls to Sag Harbor, an old whaling village.

They were sitting outside an ice cream shop overlooking the marina, eating sundaes in spite of the changing weather. Clouds had begun to gather during their hour ride from home and now a light wind had kicked up, causing a slight chill.

"Truth-telling is essential to poetry," Caro explained.

Beatrice said, "I don't know about poetry, but sometimes I think I'm being honest with myself about something, and then I figure out later I wasn't. Like Holden Caulfield in *The Catcher in the Rye*, he never gets it."

"It's truthfulness as you know it. It's rare—and I think most always impossible—to identify. Sometimes people tell lies just out of habit."

Caro offered Beatrice a supportive smile of her opinion, and then slid her tongue along her spoon, catching up strawberry syrup with a slurp. The girls looked at each other and rolled their eyes.

Their screwed-up faces reminded Caro of Abby at their age, and she wondered if her daughter still made that kind of face. The thought spun itself into a fragment for a poem—*so far the journey that creates lapses in the mind's eye*. The words, *of one once loved,* came to mind. Her love for Abby wasn't in the past. Even what Zach and Marcie had done didn't eradicate the love that Caro had so freely, if not carelessly, given. And yet the words had risen to bite her.

"What are you staring at?" Livia asked Caro.

Caro pointed toward the horizon. "My daughter, Abby, lives on the other side of the Atlantic in London. All we'd have to do is fly in a straight line from here to there and you could meet her. She would think you were wonderfully, brilliant young women. She'd be so impressed she'd take you around to all the famous places—Oxford, Buckingham, Westminster..."

"That's not true. You're making fun of us," Beatrice complained.

Livia punched her friend in the arm. "No, she's not. She's constantly telling us we're all those things."

"It's true. No fooling," Caro confirmed.

"Wow," Beatrice puffed up her chest.

"Surprise, everyone!"

Caro spun around to see Nina jogging toward them. At the sound of her aunt's voice, Livia grimaced.

Nina set her camera and shopping bags on the seat next to her niece. "Hey, you."

"I thought you were in New York City with Tommy," Caro said.

"When Beatrice's mom said you'd come here I had the best idea so I sent him alone." Nina took matching Westhampton Beach T-shirts out of a shopping bag and said to the girls, "Aren't these fun? I thought since you don't have any keepsake photos of each other, we can take some on the water wearing these. What do you think, Beatrice?"

"Cool," she said and took one of the shirts Nina offered.

"Where are we supposed to change?" Livia asked, her voice soured by her aunt's intrusion.

"Use the bathroom inside," Nina said. "I think we should shoot along the pier. Rocks, this time, not sand. Plus, the shacks on the far shore add an interesting backdrop."

Livia swatted her T-shirt on the tabletop as she got up. She approached the shop door and read loudly, "'Bathrooms are for customers only.'"

Nina sighed. "You *are* a customer and you're only changing your top, for God's sake. They *intend* that sign to prevent the general public from going in and out with dripping bathing suits. Now get a move on."

The girls came out of the shop in a few minutes and walked with Caro and Nina to the pier. Twenty minutes later, frustrated by her aunt's poking and prodding, Livia complained, "You're making this into a formal shoot."

Nina ignored Livia and said to Beatrice, "Stay just like that," as she moved Beatrice into profile on a driftwood log so that she was gazing at Livia with her arm around Livia's shoulders and her hand in her friend's lap. To her niece she barked, "Stop squirming."

"Did you hear what I said?" Livia shot back.

Nina homed in on Beatrice. "Are you having fun?"

"A blast. No one *ever* takes my picture except my mom."

"I'm cold," Livia said.

Nina cupped Livia's chin, squeezing it meanly. "Did you hear that? Be cooperative."

Nina shot a dozen pictures. After reviewing them, she groaned in dissatisfaction. With the camera suspended by a wide strap around her neck, she fiddled with their positions until at last she breathed out a confident, "Yes" and made one last set of adjustments.

The girls sat side by side, facing forward except for their heads, which Nina tilted so that their temples touched. She placed Beatrice's right hand on Livia's thigh and Livia's left hand on Beatrice's thigh. Their opposite hands hung parallel to their bodies.

"Perfect," Nina breathed, capturing what appeared to be a human study in light and dark: Livia's goldenness contrasted with Beatrice's coffee coloring; Livia's delicacy compared to Beatrice's coarseness; Livia's sullenness versus Beatrice's lightness.

As a writer, Caro often *saw* her poetic images in her mind before she gave them form on paper. Like performance art, they were organic manifestations of the work.

As much as Livia loathed the camera, her body responded favorably, seeming to seek out the lens, tracking it with elegant but subtle movements. Even the small gestures—the lowering of her eyes, a barely perceptible movement of her lips, a forward bend in the shoulders—bore an unconscious coquetry.

Caro wrapped her arms around herself, a defense against the dropping temperature of the salty air that sank into her bones. Once before, Caro had felt chilled to her inner depths, scuba diving in a quarry known for its whirlpools of icy water that ran in from the Allegheny Mountains and could freeze a human in seconds.

Caro had relied on expert aquatic navigation to negotiate her way around the whirlpools and find the safety of shore. Nonetheless, afterwards she felt that somehow she had tricked Mother Nature in spite of her skill because the odds were that she should not have made it out without incident.

That afternoon in Sag Harbor, with Livia the singular subject of her focus, Caro was ill-equipped to stave off the dangers of nature and she knew that sooner or later she would drown in the whirlpools of her own desires—although she doubted those waters would be cold.

Time to plant tears, says the almanac.
The grandmother sings to the marvelous stove
and the child draws another inscrutable house.

~Elizabeth Bishop

CHAPTER FOURTEEN

Sometimes Caro envisioned Nina and Tommy's reactions should they discover her feelings toward their niece. She imagined Nina screaming, *'pervert,'* and Tommy raising his hand to slap her. During those times, Caro felt the sweat slither down her back before she was able to erase the images from her mind.

Caro and Livia were in the sunroom, their favorite place of study. Caro had turned off her cell phone and had drawn the drapes and shutters. Tommy was at the salon and Nina was in East Hampton for *Premier Living Magazine,* shooting a spread on Martha Stewart.

Livia read from Elizabeth Bishop's *The Collected Prose.* She loved the story called "The Country Mouse," an autobiographical sketch of the events following Bishop's father's death and her mother's being committed to an insane asylum. Reading the rags-to-riches tale, Livia cried at the part where the five-year-old Elizabeth is taken from the nurturing Nova Scotia home of her maternal grandparents to board the train that takes her to Boston to live under the supervision of her father's austere, wealthy parents.

Caro chose the collection thinking that Livia would probably react emotionally. Bishop's plight was so comparable to Livia's own situation, left (as it were) on her aunt's doorstep to spend the summer. Caro hoped that reading about Bishop's pain would help Livia find expression for her own hurt.

Livia read aloud from the story, "'I had been brought back unconsulted and against my wishes to the house my father had been born in, to be saved from a life of poverty and provincialism, bare feet, suet puddings, unsanitary school slates, perhaps even the inverted Rest of my mother's family.' What are the *inverted Rest?*" she asked Caro.

"Reading, writing, and arithmetic without the *w* in writing or the *a* in arithmetic."

"Do you think she still would've been a famous poet if she had stayed in Nova Scotia with the poor family?"

"It's hard to know, isn't it? There are many writers who never had a day of formal education. Ernest Hemingway is a famous example. From high school he went to work as a reporter for a Kansas City newspaper and then served in the ambulance corps as soon as the World War broke out."

Livia put her book down. "Mom already has my college picked out for me."

"Where?"

"Vassar. She started but never finished because she married Dad. Anyway, I want to go to NYU like Aunt Nina. She took me in May during their film festival. We sat in Washington Square watching the mimes juggling and musicians strumming their banjos and guitars. There was a clown on stilts and I threw coins in a performer's hat after he played "Annie" on his harmonica for me." Livia ended her story with a small sigh, her eyes shining with the memory of it.

The doorbell rang and Caro's frustration came out in an expletive under her breath. It was Tommy.

"What's up?"

He peered into the interior past Caro, and seeing Livia on the floor motioned for Caro to step outside. He produced a negative between his thumb and index finger. "Do you know about this?"

Caro held the negative up to the light. It was of Livia and Beatrice. Beatrice wore a tank top and jean shorts and knelt in back of Livia, who sat back on her heels, her head leaning against Beatrice's chest. Livia wore a white, ruffled cotton skirt and a garland of white flowers. Beatrice's hands rested on the flowers that covered Livia's breasts.

Caro shook her head. "I've never seen this one."

Tommy plucked the negative from her. "Do you know where she is?" he asked. He was glaring; he seemed to mean Nina.

"In East Hampton on a Martha Stewart interview—"

"That's strange." Tommy's voice smacked of sarcasm. "I got a call from the editor of the magazine, yelling because the replacement Nina arranged for never showed and Stewart is furious at being stood up."

"She never meant to do the shoot?" Caro asked.

"Would seem not. She's not answering her cell. Do you have any idea where she might've gone?"

"No," Caro said, but she suspected Nina had gone to New York to meet with John Straub, the director of the National Center for Photography, regarding the exhibition.

Tommy slackened his shoulders in an effort to compose himself. "I would be worried that something happened to her had I not found this on the floor outside her darkroom."

"Is there anything I can do?"

"Do you mind keeping Livia overnight? I'm assuming Nina will get home at some point and I don't want Livia hearing us argue over her. She's at the center of what's between me and Nina. By the same token, it's not about her at all."

"Not to worry. I'd love to have her," Caro said.

Tommy followed Caro back inside. "Hey you, you feel like camping here tonight? Your aunt and I are going out and won't be home until late."

"Fine with me," Livia said, and sidled up to Caro. "We'll have a movie marathon?"

"Anything," Caro replied and meant it from a place in her heart no one before had touched.

Hands off! I do not molest what I photograph, I do not meddle and I do not arrange.

~DOROTHEA LANGE

CHAPTER FIFTEEN

Nina's olive skin coloring and black garments were a vivid contrast to the chalk white and glass walls in the exhibition hall. She stood rigid, an outward show of the nervous tension that rocked her stomach as she watched the maintenance crew hang her collection: eighteen fourteen-by-twenty-inch photographs suspended on a partition hanging by chain links from the high, domed ceiling. In an area that favored overly large works, the modest dimensions, coupled with the intimate subject matter, provided their own drama.

Before today, she'd been so sure of her work, so trusting about her success. Now, seen against the backdrop of the other exhibitors, her confidence drained, and for the first time Nina really pondered how she'd cope with failure.

John Straub came up behind her. "It's nerve-wracking I know," he said. "It helps to keep in mind that you got this far. It's trite to say, but that in itself is impressive," he added with an encouraging smile.

"Thank you," Nina said. "Is it also trite to say that I have a lot at stake?"

"I have heard that once or twice. In your case, your work is good and it's controversial. Should be a winning combo. Critics love controversy because it gives them a heap of journalistic fodder."

After John left, Nina remained staring up at a black and white representation of Livia kneeling inside a hand-drawn circle on the smooth sand of an outgoing tide. Her hair clung to her shoulders and upper arms in knotty, wet strips, like seaweed. Her eyes reflected the recession of the shadowy swells as she pointed to a place on the horizon beyond the boundary she'd inscribed in the sand.

❧

That night Nina pleaded with Tommy. "I'm not a bad person. And there's nothing immoral about those photographs. They're beautiful. They're art. For the first time in my life I've produced genuine art. If you saw how other people view them, you'd understand."

Normally slow to anger, Tommy didn't know how to control the frenzy that rocked his insides. "You're suggesting that I go to the exhibition, knowing how I feel. That takes balls, Nina. Real balls."

"Yes, go for me." Nina looked him in the eye and defied him.

"You're cocksure of yourself because John Straub is in love with your work. Fuck! All the goddamn critics probably will be, for Christ's sake! Now tell me. Where does your love for me come into this—for my opinion, for Livia?"

"If you gave *any* thought to Livia you'd attend the opening. And as for your opinion, it doesn't count. This isn't about you. That's what you don't get."

"No, that's what *you* don't get," he said and stomped out, leaving the front door swinging open behind him.

Minutes later Nina heard his car skid out of the driveway. She ran up to her bedroom where the quietest cry came out of her, a muffled yelp. On her nightstand was a photo taken at the New York Botanical Garden. Tommy, Livia, and herself wore silly grins, trying to hold back from laughing at the couple who took the photo: a bulging, burly man who wore a hearing aid and his short, effeminate, overbearing partner who yelled instructions that went unheard.

Nina's body sagged. Only with great effort did she remove her shoes and slide fully dressed into the dark security of the bedcovers where she consoled herself in a low, broken voice. "I haven't done anything wrong."

When Tommy returned home he stood for long minutes staring at his sleeping wife. He remembered another time, thirteen years ago that he had watched her in repose. It was the night she'd told him she was pregnant. They'd been married for six years, and both were nearing forty. They'd been trying to have a baby since their honeymoon.

Unable to sleep, he had sat on the chaise lounge opposite their bed, which had a view into what would be the nursery, and mentally decorated the room in green and pink.

Inexplicably, he'd imagined a daughter. He'd promised himself he'd be a good father, loving and attentive, as his dad had been to him, and had pictured himself rocking his infant girl after a midnight feeding.

Nina, on the other hand, had gone past wanting to be a mother. During their years of trying to get pregnant, she'd fought depression by putting all of her energy into her career, and with her first exhibition just months away, she'd said to him, "No way, I want a baby. It's too late for that."

"Please think about it at least," Tommy had begged. "It's not too old having kids at our age."

Two days later, without further discussion, Nina had the abortion. When she told him, he'd packed a suitcase and left, but only for a week. In spite of her betrayal, he still loved her and somehow managed to stuff his wounded feelings into the far reaches of his psyche.

Until now. Livia was the same age his daughter would have been. He loved Livia, and thinking about her in terms of the child he'd never had brought both a renewed anger at Nina and an acute urge to protect Livia, emotions that upended his normal sense of fairness and logic.

When he stormed out, he'd driven to a local hangout, prepared to let a couple of martinis dull his temper. But he wasn't a drinker and instead headed for the town beach where he sat on a picnic table and gave himself over to the anesthetizing music of the surf and the quiet radiance from a half-moon.

What he concluded was that he couldn't know for sure what side of right or wrong he was on anymore. In addition, that morning after Nina told her niece about the exhibition, elaborating on where and when it was going to be held, Livia had sought her uncle out.

"I'm not sure I'll be there," he'd said to her.

"But why? Please, Uncle Tommy, you have to. I don't want to talk to a lot of people if you're not going to be there with me."

"Maybe," was all he could say, and then felt his heart sink when she turned away, clearly disappointed.

There came a time when the risk to remain tight in the bud was more painful than the risk it took to blossom.

~ANAIS NIN

CHAPTER SIXTEEN

On Friday night the exhibition previewed for news media, critics, and a short list of invited guests. As John Straub predicted, Nina's collection caused a range of uproar that at one end hailed her as "Manhattan art scene's best-kept secret" to her detractors, one of whom, after a Q & A session, labeled her a "picture-taking deviant in a skirt."

"How do you explain your use of nudity?" the critic asked, his voice sharp.

Nina took a thoughtful pause before she replied. "There is no nudity," she said.

"Excuse me," he retorted. "What about "Summer Flowers" or "Innocence?"

"In the first photograph, she's wearing shorts and a garland around her neck. In the latter, her back is turned and she has on a sarong. There is nothing more immoral in any of my photographs than what most of you here with children have in your family albums."

"How would you know?" a woman asked. "Your bio states you have no children."

Nina reached for composure. "I was a child with a family who took pictures. It's the perspective you're viewing from, and the intention you're looking at them with, that determines what you see."

Forty-five minutes later, Nina left the conference room, exhausted, with the other five exhibitors, and relieved that Tommy hadn't been there to hear the backlash. He'd offered to take her and she'd declined, knowing that his attendance at the formal opening the next day would be tense enough.

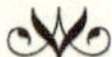

On Saturday afternoon Tommy escorted Nina, Livia, and Caro up the steps of the National Center for Photography. The doors were just opening. Tommy led Livia through, glimpsing the banner that advertised the artists included in the "Changing Faces of Youth" exhibition. Caro hung back with Nina.

The photo of Nina reflected the uncharacteristic seriousness and steadfastness with which she had pursued her ambition of producing work worthy enough to be hung among the likes of Sally Mann and Annie Leibovitz. Her facial expression hinted at her inexperience with being in the limelight: her eyes wide, her cheeks slightly flushed at the curve of the bone.

Caro took Nina's arm as they negotiated the growing crowd of guests headed for the Rockefeller Room where the exhibition was staged. Nina's series was thematically grouped under three titles: "On the Seashore," "Two Friends," and "Growing Up."

Almost immediately a small crowd clustered around Nina, pushing Caro to the outer edges of the circle. She welcomed the opportunity to be out of Nina's spotlight and move within sight and earshot of Livia and Beatrice, who'd come with her mother. She homed in on Livia, who kept shaking her head in disgruntlement.

"What's your problem," Beatrice said to her friend.

"I don't want to be here with all these people staring at us. Think they'd never seen pictures of girls before," Livia groused.

"You're such a ninny sometimes. This is the coolest thing ever," Beatrice said.

Livia ground her shoe on the floor before walking with Beatrice to the next photograph titled "Study in Dark & Light."

Beatrice waved excitedly to Nina, who smiled at her enthusiasm.

Phyllis arrived. She found Tommy only after viewing the exhibition. "I didn't know Nina was a portrait photographer. She's quite impressive."

"That's what everyone is saying."

"You sound as if you don't agree," Phyllis said.

"I agree with the breadth of her talent. Not with the theme," Tommy said.

"Why?"

"You don't find it provocative?" Tommy escorted Phyllis to the last picture in the grouping under "Growing Up."

Nina must have taken it the night of Phyllis's party because Livia had on the sea-green sundress and held the posy she'd given Phyllis as a thank-you for her invitation. She was half-sitting, half-laying on a chaise with her arm slung over her head; her dress revealed the length of her leg to her thigh; a single strap of her sandal had come undone. Livia's face slanted toward her left shoulder. In profile, her lips fashioned a soft "O" and her long eyelashes graced the tops of her cheekbones.

Tommy lowered his voice. "This is what I mean. And what about how Beatrice is portrayed? Poor kid. Beauty and the beast."

"Tommy!" Phyllis scolded. "What a rude thing to say."

"I'm only saying how it is. If anyone's *rude*, it's Nina. She's the one with the camera."

"Listen to me," Phyllis said. "Nina's your wife. And she's an artist. Sometimes the two don't mix. Unfortunately, you don't get one without the other—"

"With all due respect, you don't understand."

"Hear me out, Tommy. As for Beatrice, that *poor* kid, as you call her, is ecstatic to have pictures of herself hanging in a museum. What kid wouldn't? Plain Jane or not?"

"Livia," Tommy said.

"Livia's a beauty. Nina captured that," Phyllis said.

"And miserable. She hasn't smiled once since we left home."

Phyllis snickered. "Livia is being a little tyrant. And with you, she knows she has her Uncle Tommy in the palm of her hand."

"You're making her out to be a manipulative brat," Tommy argued quietly.

Phyllis pointed to the girls who were only a few yards away. Beatrice seemed like she was trying to say something to Livia who kept turning away in a huff. Finally, Livia left her friend to go by Caro.

"If the shoe fits," Phyllis said. "Everyone confirms she's special, particularly you and seems like Caro as well."

Livia asked Caro, "Can we go home?"

"I don't think so."

"Seems like we've been here for ages," Livia whined.

"I know," Caro said, and stroked Livia's back.

"Besides, all this is, is to make Aunt Nina famous. She told Uncle Tommy that if people like these pictures, she has an idea to photograph girls in India, and Africa, and..." Livia cut her sentence off.

Caro faced Livia. "That's a wonderful idea. What's wrong?"

Livia's eyes swam and grew larger but she held on. "The next time my mother goes away and my—my aunt is somewhere else in the world, then where do I go?" Livia stuttered in a cracking voice, like glass crunching underfoot. "I—I'll get sent away, to some school somewhere."

"Your mom hasn't said anything to you, has she?"

"I know. I just know! George's kids are in a boarding school. And I don't care that a lot of kids go. I don't want to. I want a home to go to every day, not once a month." Livia threw her arms around Caro and cushioned her face in the fold of Caro's elbow.

Caro felt the patches of moistened skin from Livia's tears, and wanted to cry along with her. Instead, she collected her breathing and then pried the blonde head out of its hiding place. With the flats of her thumbs she dried Livia's cheeks while she offered words of comfort. "What might happen months from now, is then. For now, this moment in time, you're in safekeeping. I, for one, am not going away. For sure neither are Aunt Nina or Uncle Tommy. Who would your uncle go clamming with?"

Livia released a small smile, like a flower budding.

"What have you ladies been up to?" Tommy asked.

Caro winked at Livia. "Girl talk."

"Well, I have some news. John Straub just informed Nina that the owner of a gallery in SoHo wants to meet with her tomorrow morning so I'm making reservations at the Regency for tonight; we'll get whatever personal things we need at the hotel boutique. What do you think? We can all stay or I can go back to Long Island with you."

"My choice would be to go back and let Nina take care of business," Caro said.

"Me, too," Livia agreed.

"All right," Tommy said.

Caro grabbed his arm. "Tommy, why don't you stay with Nina? I'll take the car and you two can get a driver to take you back tomorrow."

"I don't know," he hesitated.

"Seriously, I don't mind. And I don't think Livia does, right?"

"I don't care, Uncle Tommy. Maybe Beatrice can come with us, too."

Tommy looked over at his wife, stunning and slim in a red dress and spiked heels that made her taller than most of the women and even some of the men. She'd confided to her husband once that the added height was self-affirming. It instilled a sense of confidence and authority in a world not meant for female photographers.

Tommy's shifting emotions about the show, about whether he should stay with his wife or go back to Westhampton, played out in the worry lines across his brow.

"Have you decided?" Nina asked him.

"I'll stay."

Nina kissed her husband at the corner of his mouth.

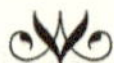

After a supper of Chinese take-out, Caro left Livia and Beatrice to moon-gaze on the beach. It was a habit they'd gotten into whenever they slept over. Counting stars, they'd explained to Caro, made them dizzy and giddy. And wasn't it great to live under such a beautiful sky!

Caro retired to her bedroom where she could monitor them occasionally. She tried to write but couldn't concentrate. Neither could she settle down to read. The day's events had taken their toll and she took aspirin for a headache. She heard

Livia come in, use the bathroom, and go out again. She paced around her bed and then settled in the wingback chair that took up the tight corner next to the window and had only a canted view of the beach.

Caro saw them perched on their blanket, illuminated by a moonbeam the size of the Coney Island boardwalk. Squirreling their toes in the sand, they leaned on their elbows, their faces to the night sky.

Taking pleasure in their apparent peacefulness, Caro observed for more minutes than she normally would. She began to notice Beatrice sneaking sidelong glances at Livia. Each time, Caro saw Beatrice rest her eyes on her friend longer. One half-second. Then two. And then Beatrice tapped Livia's shoulder and when Livia turned, Beatrice kissed her on the lips.

Caro nearly fell off the bed. She told herself that it was wrong to spy on them. Still she twisted her body from the chair and drew close to the window until her mouth was pressed against the glass, just as Beatrice kissed Livia again.

Caro stood trembling, dry-mouthed, her lips quivering with the pulse of desire that drummed inside her and created a white heat that coursed through her body.

They didn't *do* anything else. Except for the two kisses, Beatrice touched Livia only to pull her up by her hands when they were ready to come in.

Caro paced the limited pathway around the bed, stopping short when minutes later there was a knock on the door, and Livia spoke. "We're going to bed now. Are you coming out to say goodnight?"

Caro wet her lips and breathed deeply, her reply riding on the tail of her exhalation. "I have a headache, so unless you need something…"

"That's okay. We're good," Livia said and went back down the hallway to rejoin her friend.

There are chapters in every life which are seldom read and certainly not aloud.

~CAROL SHIELDS

CHAPTER SEVENTEEN

Somehow Caro made it through the rest of the night and the next day without letting on how jealous she was of Beatrice. She cursed herself for her feelings. At the same time, she was powerless to release them.

Livia and Beatrice left at noon. When Nina came to the door to collect them, Caro had lied and said she was going to the city for a couple of days to meet with her editor. Even as she spoke, however, recollection of the girls kissing kept morphing in her mind until the image became unbearable and she couldn't look Nina in the face. It wasn't Beatrice kissing Livia anymore. It was her—Caro.

She drove away the following morning after the crunch of weekend husbands returned to their city jobs and domiciles. Her car sped toward the smog-ridden horizon. After weeks of looking upon the great Atlantic in all its mercurial moods and at its vast, heavenly blue counterpart, the drive through the Midtown tunnel that dumped her in Manhattan made the phlegm rise in Caro's throat and her chest tighten.

The sidewalks seemed dirtier; the gutters more littered. The buildings appeared taller and more intrusive in their gray concreteness. She swerved into a parking space and slammed her hand on the steering wheel. Her heart hammered so hard she felt as if any second it was going to burst through her chest in one lethal explosion.

"I can't stay here," she groaned. "I just can't." She felt suffocated by the city. Then again, the events that summer—Marcie's death, and betrayal...even her love for Livia seemed designed to suck the air out of her and destroy her.

She would accomplish at her apartment what she wanted, and then be gone again to the open spaces of sand and beach.

Caro hadn't been in the apartment since she'd discovered Zach's affair with Marcie. Sometimes upon waking, she envisioned her reaction to seeing the memorabilia of the three of them that decorated the walls, tabletops, and bookcases. At those times, Caro grieved with each word of love and yearning that she supposed might have passed between them. Now, as she drove closer, her knuckles whitened on the steering wheel.

Caro lived on the top floor of a 1900s brownstone. She'd purchased the apartment the year after Zach died because she'd wanted a change. In a sentimental decision, she chose a location on the Hudson River almost exactly opposite the point where they had their home on the New Jersey side.

The New York skyline was an infinitely better view. But from her present vantage point, she liked the idea of gazing across the narrow waterway and being able to identify places she and Zach had frequented as a couple. The Steamboat Restaurant and Chappy's Grill had been their favorites.

Standing in her living room, looking out at the familiar landmarks, her memories now led only to suspicion. The times Marcie had joined them for steaks at Chappy's and Caro had gone home early to work. Had Zach and Marcie gone to the movies as they'd claimed? Or had they raced to her place for quick sex?

When she'd given out-of-town readings, had they acted like a couple? It suddenly occurred to her that Chappy himself and Roger, the maitre d' at The Steamboat must have known about them. She'd never again be able to go to either of those places without giving herself away. She'd not be able to face them without blurting out, "Did you know?"

Caro found herself grinding her palms together and biting her bottom lip as she looked around the room. The confluence of memories overwhelmed her. The fireplace mantel was flush with photographs. On the side table was one of Zach escorting Marcie onto the ferry at Fire Island.

Caro reached for it, intending only to try and decipher Zach's expression. She wanted some kind of clue that corroborated the truth. But as she drew the likeness of his face closer to her, the anger ignited and she flung the picture across the room, knocking over a picture of her and Marcie.

Carvings, baskets, and miniatures—Caro moved methodically around the apartment dumping the once-treasured gifts into a garbage bag. She cringed every time she heard the objects crack and break. At the same time, the destruction felt liberating, especially when she dragged her booty down the hall and dumped it into the trash bin.

With the exception of a photo of Abby that she was taking back with her, the remaining ones of Caro, Zach, and Abby, she put away for safekeeping in the storage closet with Abby's name on it. Next she dusted and fluffed pillows. Then she sat at her desk with Abby's picture in front of her and dialed her number in London.

"I'm home in Manhattan," she said to her daughter. "I just got finished packing up all the pictures of you, me, and Dad and I'm calling to know if there is any special item you want me to send you. I'm locking the place up for awhile."

"Why now—you only have another month on your rental," Abby said. The depressed sound of her mother's voice sounded alien to her daughter.

"Maybe I'll stay on the Island for the rest of my sabbatical. Rent a year-round place. I haven't thought ahead that far. I only know I can't live in this place again."

"I can't think of anything. I took what I wanted when I came here," Abby said. "Mom, you don't sound right. You shouldn't have gone to the apartment by yourself. You could've phoned one of your friends from school to go along."

"And have to tell them my sorry story?" Caro said. "I don't think so. Anyway, it's done now."

Abby had to moisten her lips before she said, "I've been thinking, I don't want you to see me anymore as being all like Dad."

"What brought this on?" Caro asked.

"Since you found out about his affair. He really hurt you and I never saw it that way before. I...I always believed you deserved how he treated you."

"Thank you, Abby. Telling me that means the world to me."

"Phillip accused me of being controlling," Abby confided. "Said that I wanted everything neat, that I didn't know what love was. And I was wondering if that was part of the reason why you didn't want to know what was going on between Dad and Marcie? I always saw you as being selfish...but, were you afraid, Mom?"

"I didn't know before, but yes, I guess it was out of fear more than anything else." Caro heard the muffled mewling of Abby weeping, the sound of which made her tear up as well. "What about Phillip now?"

"I told him he was wrong and sent him away," Abby said.

"Are you going to call him up and get him back?"

"I'm going to try," Abby said.

Caro looked around at all of the surfaces now empty of their accessories, and said, "Abby, I want to leave now. One thing before we hang up, instead of comparing yourself to Dad or me, be you. I'm sure that's the person Phillip is longing to meet."

"I love you, Mom."

"Me, too, Abby."

When finally Caro locked up the apartment, she knew that one day in the future she would recall this leave-taking: the thud of the ancient elevator as it reached her floor; the tinny click of the key in her door, the dense snap of the deadbolt. She would remember. It signaled the moment she knew that her life, as she knew it, was over.

On the way back, when Caro checked traffic in the rearview mirror she caught sight of her face from her nose to the top of her forehead. She grumbled over the gray roots along her hairline and the white stubby hairs that had invaded her eyebrows, making them look bristly. Her eyes had lost their sheen some time in the early morning hours while she had tossed helplessly and sleeplessly in bed.

She keyed in Tommy's salon on her cell phone. "Tommy, please."

"He's with a client. May I help you?"

"This is Caro Barrone. I need appointments for a color, cut, and facial for tomorrow."

"One moment," the receptionist said. When she came back on the line, she said, "Sorry, his first available is not until next week. The aesthetician is available for the facial though. Would you like me to make the bookings?"

"No, I wouldn't. I want you to please tell Tommy that I have an affair to attend and have to come in tomorrow," Caro insisted.

"He's booked solid, ma'am. Perhaps someone else?"

Caro was just about to argue when she heard Tommy's voice in the background, and then the transfer of the call to his extension.

"Caro, I'll slot you in but I'm fitting you in between clients, so be prepared to wait."

The receptionist was on again before Caro had a chance to thank him. "One p.m., Ms. Barrone. See you then."

When Caro hung up, she realized somewhat guiltily the many small lies she had told over the summer to be in Livia's company—just as now, leading Tommy to believe she had somewhere important to go. In the next instant, however, she reasoned that the prize of keeping Livia near was well worth the dishonesty.

Twas this deprived my soul of rest,
And raised such tumults in my breast;
For, while I gazed, in transport tossed,
My breath was gone, my voice was lost...

~Sappho

CHAPTER EIGHTEEN

Several days later, Caro, Nina, Tommy, and Livia piled into his Hummer and drove to a strip of beach between Long Island Sound and the ocean, a perfect picnic spot accessible only by boat or all-terrain vehicle. Locals usually came out midweek for moonlight suppers or overnight campouts. A dozen families were already there but since the beach extended for half a mile, Tommy was able to park a fair distance beyond the last camper.

He dragged out pails and rakes, then he and Livia sloshed along the shoreline and into ankle-deep water where they began dragging their rakes through the sandy bottom in search of clams.

"I see you don't have a camera with you," Caro said to Nina as they watched Tommy and Livia at their task.

"One of my concessions. No family pictures unless pre-approved." Nina coiled her hair in a tail and threw it over her shoulder in a gesture of dismissal. "Guess we've had enough for a while anyway."

Nina set about lighting the fire and putting the lobster pot to boil while Caro dug in the food hamper for the condiments and tableware. "I might have an offer from someone to buy the "Growing Up" series. The gallery owner I contracted with got in touch this afternoon with the news."

"Full asking price?" Caro asked.

"Incredible, but yes. Six thousand for the individual portraits and thirty-six for each series. John says it's a steal. Can you imagine? My lighthouse series in total brought in one-tenth of that."

"Does Livia know they're up for sale?" Caro asked?

"She said good riddance or some such thing," Nina said as she fanned the fire.

Livia squealed in delight and the women looked over to where Tommy was waving a crab at her. Livia started to retreat and kicked at the surf, until she fell and came up laughing.

"Think she means what she says?" Caro asked.

"I guess so. Why?"

Caro moved around to stand next to Nina. "I want to put in an offer for all three series."

Nina screwed up her shoulders. "What did you say? Never mind, I heard you. But why?"

Caro wished she could tell Nina the whole truth…confess to her how she could dally over each fragment of feature that made up Livia's face, or the dip and line of muscles and bone that composed her body. How when Caro lay in bed she dreamed of having Livia wrapped in her arms.

Caro said, "She's become very special to me, and I want to do something special in return."

"I can appreciate your motives, Caro. A lot of money is involved though. I mean, to be blunt, can you afford it?"

"I'm rich enough."

Nina's eyes widened. "Wow! I never figured. Then I guess we have a deal."

"We have a deal!" Caro cried. "Thank you, Nina."

"This means the world to me, you know that," Nina said, and after a moment of silent exchange of gratitude with their eyes, they embraced.

Nina asked, "What are your plans for them?"

"I want to talk to Carmen about eventually putting them in a trust for Livia. In the short term, I don't know yet. We'll figure something out together. As for telling Livia, I realize how sensitive she is about the photos. I'd still like her to know."

Nina nodded. "I'll talk to Tommy tonight. Unless he has an objection, come for supper tomorrow and we'll make it a low-key affair."

❧

That evening at Caro's house, Livia popped *Harry Potter and the Chamber of Secrets* into the DVD player. "It's the rage of the literary world," Livia had told her when Caro balked. "You're the only person alive not to have watched at least *one* Harry Potter movie."

Having seen both its predecessors twice, Livia explained the necessary plot details to Caro, who was surprised by how much she enjoyed the ingenuity of the story.

"No wonder Rowling's a billionaire," Caro said afterward.

Caro was on the sofa. Livia was lying on her back on the floor, snug in an oversized sweatshirt against the cool breezes coming in through the opened windows.

Livia spread her arms. "It's hard to even imagine that much money."

"I agree. She's the only woman in literary history to reach those numbers."

"Do poets get rich?" Livia asked.

"Not usually." Caro's serenity in the pale light of the sconces made her look almost pretty, the way the shadows danced across her features. She smiled at Livia's fiscal naiveté at the same time that she recalled her own literary ambitions when she was a teen.

They couldn't see the ocean from where they were but they heard the roiling waves tumble into shore and retreat. There was a sense of assurance in the sound of the ocean. Its movement was reliable, always present, unchanging.

From her lowered position Livia said, "Did you ever write a poem that might hurt someone you cared about?"

Unprepared for the question, Caro nonetheless had an immediate answer, although it took her a few moments to gather the courage to be truthful. The incident occurred when she was first famous and still believed she had moral justice on her side, though that wasn't the case anymore.

Caro said, "Once I wrote a poem about the shortcomings of growing up in the house of Italian immigrant parents. It didn't dawn on me how hurtful the words were until my father made me read it aloud to the family."

"What happened?" Livia crept on to the couch next to Caro.

"My mother and grandmother sobbed. My sole aunt, a dozen years younger than my mother and born in New York, scolded me in Italian for an hour and then didn't let me forget the incident for three days. 'As many days as Christ was in the tomb,' she'd said. My Aunt Francesca was very religious."

"Were you sorry then that you wrote it?"

"Yes and no. I felt bad I hurt their feelings. At the same time, it's just what came out of me naturally."

"Were you born in Italy too?"

"New Jersey," Caro said.

"Hmmm, just like me." Livia drew her knees up under the hem of the sweatshirt and rested her head on Caro's shoulder.

Caro, in turn, smoothed Livia's bangs with her fingers in a repetitive motion. Livia's action reminded Caro of her daughter snuggling against her hip as a toddler. When Abby had reached Livia's age, she no longer bowed to such juvenile intimacies. Caro had missed her daughter's nearness after that.

Caro could almost taste the sea salt that glinted on Livia's skin. She inhaled the lingering scent of lavender soap she had used from Caro's bathroom. The smell mingled with the traces of it on her own body—a metaphorical blending of the flesh.

Only that morning, worn down by Livia's nagging and the high temperatures, Caro had ventured into the ocean. She didn't like the open water, fearful of the marine life that she imagined rising from the depths, circling her. She understood that shark attacks were rare. However, jellyfish, crabs, sea anemones, and lionfish were all dangerous each in their own way. Even the slime and tangle of seaweed, while not harmful, made her slap the water's surface in distaste.

Swimming alongside Livia was sweet recompense for her apprehension, and Caro relished in the sight of the pull and press of the girl's muscles, the full extension of her body. Her arms arced toward the sun, then down and through the water again, propelling her forward. Buoyed by salt water and exhilaration, her motion was effortless.

When Caro rotated and lifted her head out of the water for air, she caught snatches of Livia: the crinkle across the bridge of her nose, a sign of exertion; the fresh triangle of freckles on her cheeks; the faint trace of a scar along her jawbone, which Caro had never seen before, but now felt drawn to touch.

In shallower waters, Caro boosted Livia onto her shoulders only to let her somersault backwards with a splash. She dove underwater and came up on Livia from below, tackling her by her legs and her waist. They kicked and thrashed about, inadvertently making brief contact with body parts that were otherwise off limits, but the sensation of which Caro stored in her subconscious.

Now, the sensual recollections of her afternoon in the surf, combined with Livia's intimate repose—nestled with her head resting in the hollow of Caro's bosom—immersed Caro's face in a deep red flush. Like Alice in Wonderland, she was cascading uncontrollably down the rabbit hole.

She'd schemed to be Livia's mentor—her Socrates—guiding her in her path of true knowledge and along the journey happening upon total, perfect, and platonic love. At this moment, though, she felt no nearer to ideal love than any other kind of lust. Yet she was powerless to pull away.

Suddenly Caro felt exhausted, as if she'd engaged in some kind of strenuous activity. She glanced down at Livia, who had dozed off. A chill shot through Caro and huddling closer to the young, sweat-shirted body, she closed her eyes, her hands trembling above her, millimeters short of physical contact.

After a long while fighting against a blinding craving to kiss the soft curve of Livia's jaw line, she awakened her and took her to bed. When she went to her own room, Caro pushed open the French doors to the crash of ocean and opened her mouth, but the scream stayed inside her. She stood in the night dampness until her insides lurched with discomfort, as if she believed the chill could numb her heart-sick feelings. Nothing could save her, and she retreated to her bed, a piece of her emotional stability forever shipwrecked.

Some there are who say that the fairest thing seen on the black earth is an array of horsemen; some, men marching; some would say ships...

~Sappho

CHAPTER NINETEEN

"...b*ut I say / she whom one loves best / is the loveliest...*"

Caro let the last word sit on her tongue, enjoying the feel of it in her mouth. "Loveliest." The word made her think of skinned peaches cut into sweet morsels, or honeydew melon spooned fresh from the hollow of the fruit. They were tastes that made her mouth water and ache for more.

Caro had first come to appreciate the appeal to the senses Sappho's words held when she taught the ancient poet's writings in a workshop. She'd explained to her students how the individual words were common enough, but that how Sappho strung them together was what gave them their texture and body, and sensuality.

Nina's photographs of Livia had the same kind of rapture. She had managed to capture glimmerings of Livia's various moods: bookish seriousness, petulance, curiosity, and her athleticism, alongside her unmistakable sensuousness.

Caro recalled watching Tommy's nephew, Alex, teach Livia how to body surf. He'd come to Westhampton to visit friends but when he saw Livia get consistently dumped from her boogie board he offered his help.

A strong swimmer and surfer, Alex demonstrated the knack of determining which was the best wave to ride in on. He showed Livia how to position the board in the middle of her midriff and how to use her arms like oars and her hands like rudders.

He showed her the technique of staying on the board and riding over the crest of the wave as it rolled toward shore and then how to prevent getting hit by the board when she was thrown off.

Livia caught on quickly. After Alex went back to his friends she continued to practice, whooping and waving toward shore when she rode a wave in successfully; laughing even more when she toppled off and emerged from the surf spitting out ocean water and unwrapping seaweed from her ankles.

When Livia paddled away from shore her golden hair split her back like a brilliant shaft of light cutting a room of darkness in half. Her blonde braid came to be a symbol for the beauty and innocence that was hers; Caro named the poem she'd been writing for Livia, "The Yellow Braid." She had a wide back and well-defined shoulders for one so small-boned. It was that ocean-bound image of Livia riding the surf that inspired the beginnings of the third stanza.

A golden twist of nouns and verbs
in mute and mock display
with flying curls of
metaphors in costumed disarray.

A buried mix of hidden rhymes
so seldom sought to hear
a drawstring bag of adjectives
so difficult to bear.

A posy from a sea of verse
a weave of harvest dust
the sonnet dark, its lyrics terse…

It was curious to Caro how this poem trickled out over the summer. Usually, her verse came in a flood of words and images. She would spend days, even weeks reworking a poem, but she rarely strayed far from the initial outpouring. This poem had forced a different writing pattern on her. She concluded why after writing what she knew to be the last stanza.

Her poetry was always about trying to reveal the truth of a matter. With Livia, the deep shame that shadowed every thought of love, made it impossible for Caro to write plainly about her. And so she wrote in rhyme and metaphor, in stuttering starts and stops, with no one the wiser to her lust, but herself.

"There's no harm in experimenting." Caro snapped the color chart closed and handed it back to Tommy. She didn't care what he thought. The culture of beauty in contemporary society was of youth. It wasn't anything she'd created. Nor was there anything she could do about it.

Tommy returned the bowl of dye to his assistant, "Mix up a new batch." To Caro he said, "You are forewarned, right?"

"Yes," she said impatiently.

Half an hour later, with the stain of chestnut seeping along her forehead and neckline, Caro's cell phone rang. "Hello," she said, holding it inches away from her ear so as not to smudge it with dye.

"Mom? Are you there?"

"Abby, I can't talk now. I'll call you back."

"No, I'm afraid you won't. I thought we were okay with each other, but since you got back from the city you haven't returned any of my calls."

"We are okay, really. It's me and has nothing to do with you." Caro shut her eyes and sighed in frustration at having to be so guarded with her words. "It's been harder than I would've expected to come to terms with everything that's happened since Marcie's death."

"Maybe I should fly over to see you,—" Abby said.

"No, of course, you shouldn't. I'm fine," Caro said. She tried for assurance in her voice. "Abby, I'm in the beauty parlor packed in hair color."

"Promise you'll get back to me," Abby said.

"Later," she said. "I promise."

In reality, Caro didn't know what she was going to do. She felt like she didn't know anything anymore. Coming to the beauty parlor was a mistake; she didn't have the patience to sit quietly for any length of time so cluttered was her mind with random fears: afraid of letting something slip that might tip Abby off to her feelings about Livia, afraid that she'll lose her composure with Livia and do something—a touch or kiss that might frighten the girl away. Caro knew she'd be devastated losing Livia because of a character weakness within herself.

These thoughts made Caro pull at the neck of her robe and fidget in her seat. Her skin began to itch from the heat lamp. She waved over Tommy's assistant to find out how much more she had to endure.

Tommy himself answered when he held up his opened hand and mouthed, "Five more minutes."

Caro blew out her cheeks and huffed. All around her women sat docilely reading *Vogue* or gossiping with their neighbor. In contrast, Caro's discomfiture caused a sudden feeling of doom. Or perhaps, not suddenly. Maybe her repeated visits to

Tommy's salon and attempts at beautification and youth had been fated from the beginning.

She started to cry, first, from the inside. When the assistant settled her in the shampoo chair with her head tilted back over the rim of the sink, the tears collected on her eyelashes and rolled off her face, mixing with the lather that smelled of apricots and tangerines.

In order to know virtue, we must first acquaint ourselves with vice.

~MARQUIS DE SADE

CHAPTER TWENTY

Caro returned home, hooded and wearing sunglasses. After locking herself in and letting down the blinds, she went into her bedroom, closing the door behind her, even though no one was in the house.

The bathroom mirror confirmed her stunned reaction in the beauty salon. She'd hoped that after Tommy had washed the excess dye out and had styled her hair, the heavy coloring would have appeared less garish. It hadn't, and she was the same caricature here at home that she'd seen in his mirrors.

Beside herself with the anxiety of what she'd done despite Tommy's warning, she sent a three-word text to her daughter: *I need you*.

Almost immediately, Abby was on the phone. "Mom, I knew something's going on."

Caro sat hunched on the floor against the door. "I'm not used to this, Abby. I used to confide in Marcie. If she were here, I wouldn't be where I am in my head, ready to explode."

"Try telling me. I'm not Marcie, but at least I'm here," Abby said.

Caro took a breath. "I got my hair dyed and I look ugly and I don't know what to do about it. I'm scared because it's like...like the ugliness of my hair and my face is who I've become on the inside. Can someone have a pure heart and black soul?"

"Mom, you're talking crazy."

"I'm trying to explain," Caro said. She held her hand to her mouth, and then to the side of her face. "I made a pattern for myself this summer, going to the same places to eat, sitting on the same beach...repeating the same things because I felt too bereaved of love without Marcie to go or do differently. My way seemed safe, and all with very little effort. And then I met Livia, and she completed my narrow world. She was satisfied to stay in it with me."

There was a level of distress in her mother's voice Abby didn't recognize. "But that's good then."

"No, because I still wasn't content. I tried to be young again, look younger...to be more appealing," Caro said. "I couldn't afford to be old."

"For who?" Abby asked.

"For Livia—" A pocket of sudden nerves seemed to burst inside of Caro for mentioning Livia's name.

"Mom, she's not going to care what you look like. From the little you've said about her, she sees you as a mother figure. I'm confused why you'd be this upset. She's only a young girl, for God's sake. I would think she'd be more interested in boys than with someone who's like her mother. Besides which, you're not ugly, and I'm sure your hair is not as bad as you think."

Caro wiped at her tears and tried not to cry aloud, but couldn't hold back a small eruption of sobs.

"Mom..." was all Abby said, a reminder that she was there for her mother.

When Caro sniffled away the last of her tears, she said, "Sorry for being so melodramatic about this. I got overwhelmed."

"A lot's happened this summer that's been really upsetting. You finding out about Marcie and Dad brought it all up for me again, but at least, I knew about it already. I didn't have to deal with it for the first time."

"Abby, one more thing. I'm wanting to make amends as much as I can given that you're going to be thirty soon."

"Never too late, Mom," Abby said.

Caro heard the lift in Abby's voice and she hoped that for a moment, at least, she was smiling. "Are you jealous of Livia?"

"I tried to convince myself I wasn't. I am though. Seems like she's what you would've dreamed of in a perfect daughter," Abby said.

Caro wasn't used to being honest with Abby and she struggled against reverting to her habit of prevarication. "In the beginning, yes, I sought her out as a daughter. The emotional distance between you and me seemed so great, and I saw an opportunity to make amends for my failings as your mother. She's a poet and could easily relate, and she needed a sympathetic supporter in the absence of her own mother."

"And now?"

"Believe me when I say with all of my heart, there is no need to be jealous. I have one daughter who is not perfect, but I'm not seeking perfection. Your dad's affair was worth every second, if its discovery has opened up a new beginning between us. I never stopped loving you, Abby, not for an instant."

"I think I always knew that."

"I'm glad for that," Caro said. "So now tell me what's going on with Phillip."

"I called and asked him out on a date. We're meeting for dinner tomorrow night."

"Good girl," Caro said. "You let me know what happens. In the meantime, a big hug for you."

"Night, Mom. I love you too."

After Caro hung up from Abby, she felt an internal shudder, a loosening of nerves that had twisted around her stomach. At the same time, she had one very clear realization that made her clutch at her shirt with her fist. As much as her conversation with Abby reminded Caro of how much her daughter loved her, Caro was still alone in the matter of her heart regarding Livia.

Even now Caro imagined Livia straddling the boogie board with her arms and thighs hard from surfing; her hair bleached by the sun; her skin weathered to a Caribbean brown. When Livia dove deep and rose up again, the Greek sea goddess Tethys could have looked no more beautiful or athletic.

Caro had spent the summer seeking the solace of perfect love and learned along the way that Platonic love was for the gods. She was human.

I postpone death by living, by suffering, by error, by risking, by giving, by losing.

~Anais Nin

CHAPTER TWENTY-ONE

When the phone rang the next morning, Caro saw that it was Gwen, the owner of the house. "Hello."

"I was looking over the lease," Gwen said, "and forgotten I'd extended with you until the end of September. The problem is my situation has changed. I'm having to cut my holiday short and plan to be home in two weeks."

"But that's Labor Day," Caro said.

"I realize that. It just happens that I met a woman who turned out to be the CEO of a marketing firm in Manhattan. It was a week-long tour and by the time we returned to Rome she offered me a job."

Caro lowered the handset and stared at it in disbelief. When she raised it to her ear again, she did so gingerly, hoping Gwen would be recanting her message. She heard the voice, but not the words she wanted to hear.

Gwen was saying, " … sorry, and of course, I'll discount this month for your trouble."

Caro replied in high, stuttering tones. "I can't go back early. I—I've made plans, commitments here on the Island. It's not possible."

"I realize we have a lease. The only way I know how to honor it is if you stay on with me at the house. I just didn't know if that was something you really wanted to do."

"No. Not at all," Caro said firmly.

There was a brief silence. "I don't know what else to say except that I was hoping you would be agreeable."

Caro managed to collect herself and attempted an offensive line of argument. "It may seem like it to you because you're not hearing what you want, but I'm not the one who's being difficult. It's not realistic to think I'd be okay with cutting *my* holiday short by *three* weeks based on a decision you made on a whim."

"You're being ridiculously unreasonable, and there's no excuse for it. It's my house," Gwen retorted.

"And we have a contract. I'll spend whatever money for a lawyer I have to, to see who stays and who goes in your house. Bitch!" Caro spat.

"Attacking me is not helping," Gwen said.

"Neither is this conversation," Caro said and threw the handset onto the divan.

Even before Gwen's phone call, Caro had begun to experience brief periods of sorrow when she realized that summer was coming to an end and with it, Carmen's return from her honeymoon to get Livia. There was no way Caro would relinquish even a second of her time with Livia before that.

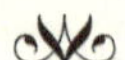

Later that evening, Caro became suddenly aware of an absolute quiet that pervaded the house in spite of the fact that Livia and Beatrice were somewhere inside. It wasn't yet eight o'clock. Yet no music blared and the forty-eight-inch TV mirrored her reflection darkly when she passed in front of it. She strained to catch any kind of noise, and heard nothing. She'd been in her bedroom, but assumed the girls would have called out to her had they left.

She walked to the side of the house where their bedrooms were and without thinking pushed open Livia's door, which was partly ajar, at the same time that she called her name.

The girls were on the bed, half-dressed; Livia was on her side facing Beatrice, her hand on Beatrice's stomach.

"Livia! Beatrice! What are you doing?"

The girls scrambled off the bed.

"Why did you come in here like that?" Livia shrieked.

Caro's grip on the door handle tightened. "I was looking for you…I didn't mean to intrude."

"We were only messing around some," Beatrice said as she drew her T-shirt over her head.

"Can you leave now? Can you *close the door*, please," Livia said, buttoning her blouse.

Caro hurried out. When she got to her bathroom, she splashed water on her feverish face—the heat arising as much for her embarrassment at walking in on them as for her desire to have been lying on the bed with Livia in her arms instead of Beatrice's.

Naturally, love's the most distant possibility.

~GEORGES BATAILLE

CHAPTER TWENTY-TWO

Fate intervened in the relationship between Beatrice and Livia. Beatrice's grandmother got pneumonia, sending Beatrice and her mother to Tucson with a plan to stay through the Labor Day weekend. Sitting in Nina's kitchen, Caro, barely concealing her glee, asked after the woman's health.

Nina poured tea. "Talking about stress, have you heard any more from Gwen?"

"She's arriving next Sunday, and staying at a friend's house. Seems that when she checked with a lawyer friend, he told her that with me having a contract, by the time the case went to civil court, I'd be long gone from the house. Still, I can hardly believe the summer's over." She let her words hang like clothes strung out on a wash line.

"Well, I have news from Carmen," Nina said.

Caro detected a slight hesitation in Nina's voice and looked up from the magazine she'd been absently thumbing through as they talked.

"Carmen wants Livia on a plane to Hong Kong on Thursday."

"Thursday! That's—that's in three days." Caro jumped from her chair.

"Livia's been on a waiting list for a private American school. The headmaster contacted them for a personal interview. The semester starts next Monday."

A frightened child would not have appeared as lost as Caro did, with her eyes wide in dismay, her jaw trembling.

"I know how close you've gotten to her but you had to know this was coming soon," Nina said, reaching for Caro's hand.

Caro backed away; she couldn't stand Nina touching her. "How long do they plan on staying overseas?"

"Two years. After that, her husband figures his company will be established to the point the family can return and then he'll make intermittent trips over alone."

Caro turned and went out the back door, then fled down the catwalk to her own house. Once there, she collapsed onto the twin bed where Livia slept, and thrust her face into the pillow. She hadn't done the linens since the last sleepover so that the smells of sea salt and the girl's scented body wash made Caro inhale deep and long. Livia! It couldn't be that in three days she would be gone. That Caro would lose her so prematurely. A low wail, in a voice she hardly recognized as her own, reverberated in her face and filled her ears.

She longed for sleep. Every night in recent weeks the young beauty had drifted across Caro's dreamscapes and metamorphosed her world. But now, even after the sun had risen toward zenith, sleep evaded her; she had to bear the full weight of Livia's impending departure in full consciousness.

At two o'clock Livia knocked at the door.

Caro sneaked behind the panel of rattan blinds and peeked at Livia shifting her feet and twirling the tail of her braid, habits of impatience. How was she going to face Livia and not cry? But she must, or allow Livia to leave thinking she wasn't home.

Caro stepped outside, her emotions appeared like script across her face.

"Aunt Nina told you."

Caro pulled the appropriate words up her throat one by one to keep from blurting out something she'd regret. "You must be … excited. Hong Kong will be so different for you."

Livia gave her a sidelong look. "Aunt Nina said you came home because you were sick."

Home. Caro turned her gaze to the ocean, the endless rotation of waves that she'd come almost to memorize. Such wasn't the case with Livia. She would be gone from her home here, never to come back.

Livia patted Caro's shoulder. "We still have three more days."

That night Livia stayed over. They'd come in early from outside. A thick fog rolled in along with hot, humid weather that made their clothes stick to their skin. After Livia took a shower, she went into Caro's bedroom to say good night. Her wet hair clung to her arms and back like slivers of gold lamé against the bronze patina of her scrubbed skin. When she flopped lengthwise on Caro's bed wearing only bikini briefs and a tank top, Caro lost her breath.

In the short space of a summer, she'd turned into the Magdalene of her poem: *fallen woman, fallen to a higher crown.* She saw her existence as a farce and yet, unable—no, unwilling—to disrupt the bliss her desire brought.

Later, after Livia was in her own bed, asleep, Caro entered her room. Livia was on her back with the sheets kicked off and her arms flung over her head.

All she knew and desired was Livia. Because if not with Livia, then with no one else. And so she knelt in Christ-like abjection, tears and sweat mingling.

Livia came awake. Her face registered only mild surprise at Caro's nearness. Even so, Caro's hand came up to her chest, and she clutched her shirt, and began wrenching it, a physical indication of an inner conflict.

"It's okay," Livia said. The soft, ambiguous words that dissolved the night space between them.

Livia had given her permission, and Caro felt herself slipping into euphoria. Her movements were slow, almost dreamlike, she felt, as she lay alongside the sweet-scented body. She stroked the dampness from Livia's forehead, the hairs along her cheekbone, then her chin, until her fingers settled on her lips.

Caro's mind no longer dictated her actions. Her heart and her desire gave her the courage to take Livia into her arms. She cradled her, and when Livia showed no resistance, she kissed her, a long and gentle kiss on the mouth that for weeks she had longed to touch.

When Caro finally drew back, she wept openly in the knowledge that for the duration of a single kiss she had found perfection. For that one long moment, she'd felt the heat of Livia's youth. She'd lost herself in the possibility of their being together and her life a yet-to-be written story instead of one already finished and critiqued.

But in the moment before, and after, she knew she had to let her go.

As if instinctively, Livia grabbed her, begging her to stay. "Please, don't leave me," she whispered, her cheek flush against Caro's. "I feel safe with you. I'll do anything you want."

"I believe you would," Caro whispered back. She began kissing Livia's head, and her face, and then caressed her body one last time before easing out of Livia's grip. A steady withdrawal was made possible only by an image Caro maintained in her mind's eye, like a rendering in one of Nina's photographs: the shoe-polish hair and liver-spotted skin, harsh reminders of her age.

"I love you, Caro." Livia's face plumped up with tears that drowned her eyes and turned her skin the color of pale ash. "Just tell me what I did wrong and I'll fix it."

"Livia, you did nothing wrong. It's me," Caro said.

"I'll write a poem for you. You like my poems . . ." Livia's words seemed to fall into a deep canyon; Caro seemed implacable. Her eyes grew large with sudden passion and she lashed out in turn: "I hate you! I hate you!"

There was a brief, startling silence between them until Livia ran out of the room. Caro heard the glass door rattle in its frame when it hit the wall. She went to the window, and in the starlight, saw Livia dash down to the beach.

She waited, calculating the time for Livia to reach home, and then dialed Nina's number.

Tommy answered. "What happened? She's a mess, but she won't say anything except that she hates you. What the hell is going on?"

"Goodbye, Tommy."

The armored cars of dreams, contrived to let us do so many a dangerous thing.

~ELIZABETH BISHOP

CHAPTER TWENTY-THREE

Caro shivered in the night air despite the heavy humidity that smudged the horizon like a dowdy gray banner, a density so powerful it hid the ocean. She trudged toward the shoreline, passing through the smoky vapors like a ghost through walls.

As she approached the water's edge, the ocean seemed to reappear, and she gazed into its boundlessness. A wave broke, steeping her feet in foam. The flood tide collected, pushing itself up the beach. In a couple of hours its level would reach high tide.

Caro lowered herself onto the sand and made figures with her fingertips in the packed wetness. She was trying to figure how she got to where she was that night: a middle-aged woman star-crossed by a child whose beauty—and very existence—could make her weep.

Except for the brief words she'd had with Tommy the night Livia ran out of her house, she hadn't spoken to anyone. Nina had come knocking at her door several times and then given up. Caro only knew the details of Livia's departure from a voicemail that Tommy left.

Caro didn't regret her actions—not the kiss, not any part of her life with Livia that summer. She'd gone in search of ideal love, and she'd found it. Not the Platonic kind that was measured only by degrees of beauty or knowledge, but rather one that acknowledged and allowed its carnal counterpart—the heat beneath the cool skin of intellect. She'd discovered that transcendent love sparkled and shone precisely because of the touch and the kiss that preceded it.

Such a complex word, *desire*. With Livia, desire was a blunt blow to Caro's being.

Caro regretted not completing her poem to Livia. Whenever she sat with it, she felt trapped in her own tongue, felt the impenetrability of language when language doesn't suffice. She'd written how many poems throughout the years? And this one … this, the most treasured of all … she'd been unable to resolve. *A posy from a sea of verse, a weave of harvest dust, the sonnet dark its lyrics terse...* Those were the last lines she'd composed.

The night sea roiled against the stiffening wind. A gasp escaped Caro's lips as a rush of cold foam hit hard against her, and she scampered to higher ground. A star dipped from the high reaches of the sky and with it a vision of Livia, the tip of her braid brushing Caro's cheek. Caro closed her eyes from the sheer joy of imagining her so near. She wanted to speak, to say Livia's name aloud one last time. Instead, the last line of the poem fell from her lips in graceful brevity. *And go she says, I must.*

Caro contemplated the simple perfection of the words for only a moment before she felt her heart open to an unexpected clarity. She'd taken emotionally from Livia, but not without giving. Throughout the weeks, she'd helped Livia through the pain of mother loss and her aunt's artistic demands. She'd shored up the girl's sense of self as a young adult and a blossoming poet. Finally, in spite of, and because of her deep love for the girl, she'd turned her away.

And go she says, I must. Caro recited the verse again and again until the words seemed to spin circles of seaweed, green and blue, wreathing their heads and linking them as one. For a time, Caro had been everything to Livia—a mother to a daughter. A mentor to a student. A lover to her beloved.

After a long while Caro rose, her limbs shaking and stiff. She paused to get her balance. As she did, she gazed backward upon the sea that she was leaving, and then forward up the beach to the house. The distance and journey of love lost with Livia seemed interminable. But in the end, she had to believe, not impossible.

www.ingramcontent.com/pod-product-compliance
Lightning Source LLC
LaVergne TN
LVHW090951080826
845145LV00003B/975